2

THE DRAGON CROWN SERIES

COURT OF DRAGONS AND VOWS

G. BAILEY

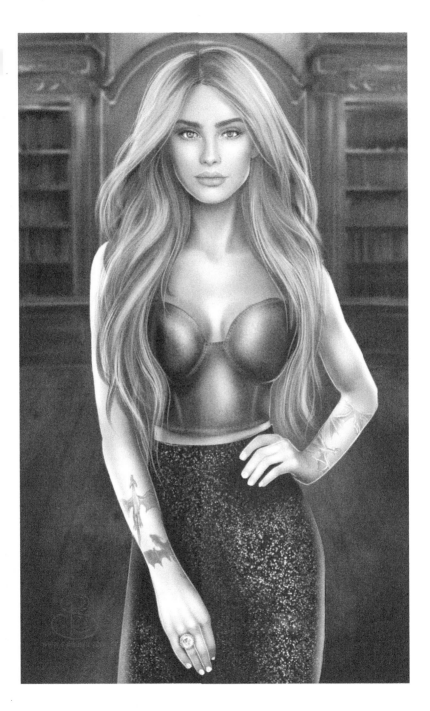

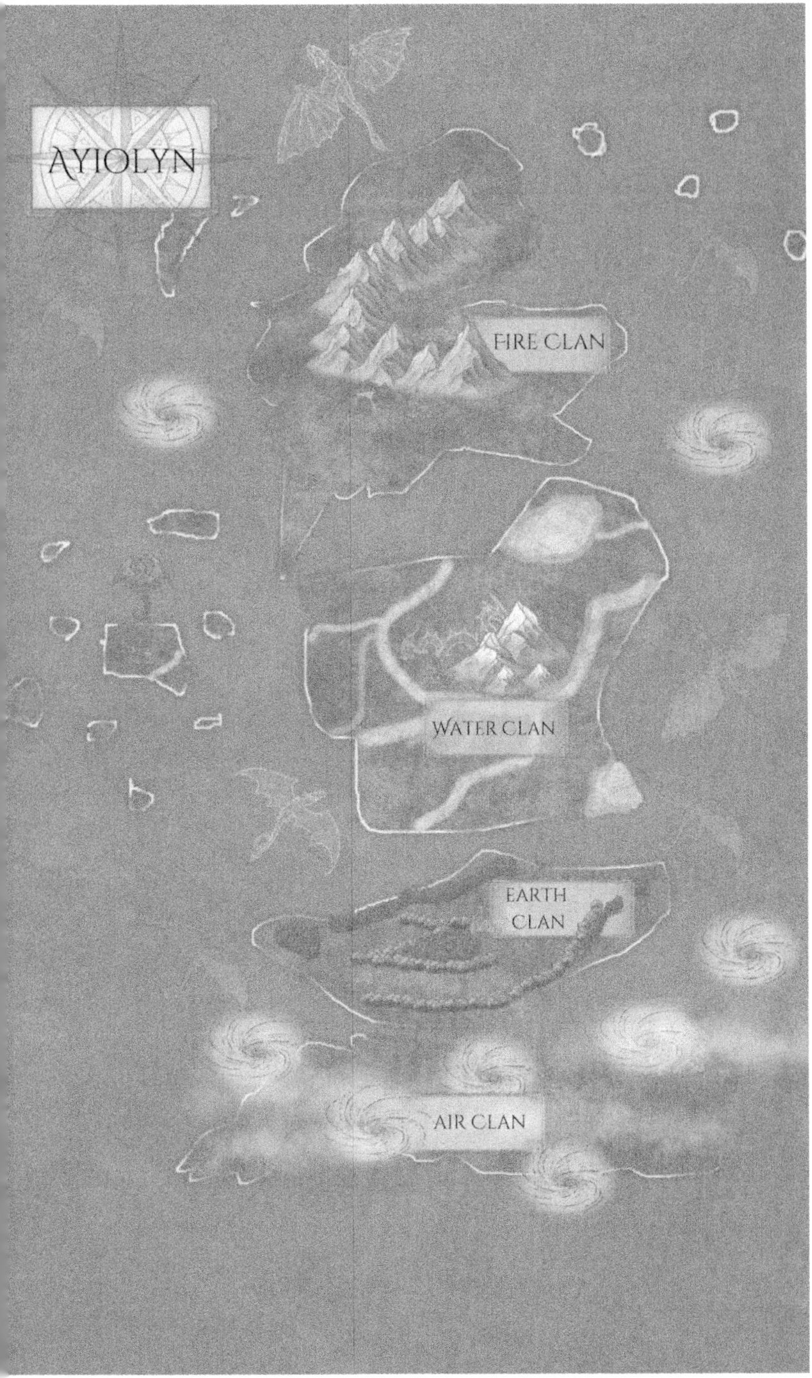
AYIOLYN
FIRE CLAN
WATER CLAN
EARTH CLAN
AIR CLAN

COURT OF DRAGONS AND VOWS

THE DRAGON CROWN SERIES

G. BAILEY

Edited by Polished Perfection

Cover by MiblArt

Artwork by Samaiya Art.
Trigger Warning: Scenes of near SA and dark themes. Feel free to
email at gbaileyauthor@gmail.com for more information, as your
mental health matters.

 Created with Vellum

CONTENTS

DESCRIPTION

The dragons of the West need riders, and to survive, I must become one of them.

After barely surviving the Dragon Crown Race, I wake up in the desert at the mercy of the dragon riders and their brutal commander. They come for me, my dragon kings, even when I didn't expect them to get out alive. The dragon kings make an uneasy alliance with the dragon riders, both with a common goal to stop the sorcerer before he gets too powerful. But they all have secrets, and they won't tell me any of them.

My new shadow dragon knew I was coming to him.

He claims I'm his destined mate…and he isn't the only one with that claim.

Old magic and Greek gods are real, and they won't stop until they have claimed Ayiolyn.

In this world of dragon riders, complicated love, and Greek gods, I need to become stronger than all of them.

I'm the princess of the fifth court, and I was born to rule.

This is a full-length enemy-to-lovers fantasy romance with dragon shifters, a badass heroine, and possessive alpha males. Perfect for fans of spicy fantasy whychoose? romance. This is book two.

CHAPTER 1

KING ARDEN OF THE FIRE COURT.

"*L*isten to her."

Groggily, I open my eyes. The effects of the drugs in my system making it near impossible to stay awake for long. Fire flickers light in the darkness, illuminating the shadows until I believe that someone is here. I lift my head, looking around. Someone is here, in the cage with me, but I can't see them. I look around the throne room from the cage I'm held in above it. The sorcerer isn't here, neither are the disloyal bastards that now serve him from our courts. Some of them bowed to him without blinking, but none of them are from my court.

I turn my head to the other three cages held near mine. Emrys, Lysander and Grayson are held within them, magically knocked out or passed out from the beatings. I've been stuck watching them from a distance, unable to help them. I'm fucking useless. Another whisper fills my ears. I'm confused as the female voice is quiet, though she's familiar and I'm not sure where I know her from. "Listen to her and find Ellelin. Please, just take the deal."

Finally, I see her, a woman in a cloak is below my cage, on her own, and she walks out without another word, and I catch only a flash of curly blonde hair. I drift off once again, probably from blood loss from the regular beatings or whatever is draining away our souls in this place. The sorcerer took our magic, and the castle locked us in. It's been months since that night, and Ellelin...I haven't stopped thinking about her. I know she survived the earth test, but she isn't in the castle anymore.

The sorcerer never speaks about her, and I never get a chance to ask before he is torturing us with his magic, in front of hundreds of our people, to make sure they don't think twice about going against his new rule. We didn't stand a chance against him without our powers and with the castle against us too.

When I wake again, I look out the window to the night sky, searching the night for her. I love her.

I think I did the second I saw her jump out of the window of the fire test. She is fierce, like the brightest part of a flame in a fire, and she was born to burn for me. I need to get to her. I need to tell her who I suspect she might be. Red light suddenly illuminates everything until it's all I can see and feel. My chains rattle as I lift my head to look around.

"Do you want to escape here, dragon king, and find your love?"

The female's voice is as soft as velvet, and I search for where she is, watching as the red light fades until there is a woman in my cage. She has long, light blonde hair that falls around her body, which is thankfully covered in a strange white dress. Her eyes are dark, like black moons, and there is something off about her. She looks my age, I'd guess, but her eyes tell me she is older than me. Something about her makes it hard to look away from her eyes, even when my dragon is roaring at me. "Who are you?"

She softly laughs, touching the cage bars. "I've been known by many names, but I liked Aphrodite the most. The goddess of love, at your service, my king." Goddess? The sorcerer told my ancestors he was a god, and look what happened when they faced a god. "I've come to help you."

"I don't want the help of any god or goddess," I snarl.

She laughs once more. "I could make you accept my deal. All men fall to me in the end, but that magic would be weak. I came here to disturb my husband, Ares. But he doesn't go by that name here, does he? The sorcerer." She sighs. "I prefer the old names."

My blood runs cold, my fire nowhere to be seen. I don't trust her, and if the sorcerer is her husband, then it's likely she is just as bad as he is. "My daughter tells me you're the most reasonable dragon king, and the one most in love. The others...it is new to them. Not to you. Love is my power, and together we can benefit each other. You want to escape here and go after your true love. I want to disturb my husband and make a home for myself here. We can't get back to our world, not yet, so how about we make a deal?"

I cross my arms, leaning back on the bars. The whole cage swings with the movement. "How about you take your husband and fuck off somewhere else?"

Her darkly tanned skin seems to glow a shade of vibrant red. "If you are the most reasonable of the kings, then I don't want to deal with the others. I cannot just fight my husband and take him away from here. That is not the deal I am offering you."

Watching her, I look past her at the night sky. I don't want to make a deal with her...but I can't get out of here myself, and being trapped here isn't going to help Ellelin or my people. At this moment in time, the sorcerer has won. His wife might be the only card we have left to play. "What do you want in return for letting me and the other kings out of here?"

Aphrodite smiles wide, and every instinct I have tells me to fucking run from her. My dragon all but roars in my head, itching to fly us away, but I can't shift, not in this cage, and I can't escape without her. "I will let you out and unlock the bind on your powers. You have six months to find your love and convince her to be your mate. That will permanently unlock your magic. The rule stands for each of you."

Jealousy and possessiveness slam hard into my chest. Ellelin is fucking mine. I won't share my mate, my queen, with them. They don't deserve her, and Lysander hates her. Grayson can't be touched, and Emrys...well, he never takes anyone seriously enough to be his. "You want us to all be her mate? Ellelin won't—"

"This is the deal," she interrupts me. "All four mates, by the end of the six months, or you all belong to me. If you can't all convince her in that time, then you will be at my side forever. I will make sure my husband is busy for the six months by making him look in the wrong places for you. This will also keep your people safe, as he will not be focused on them for the time being." She pauses with a coy smile. "Also, the Crown Race curse will be broken by your mating. She passed the test and survived. A mating with her will break my husband's magic. I will add in a sweetener, if you come back to me willingly before the six months are up, I will make sure no more of your people die."

I narrow my eyes at the goddess. It sounds too good to be true, despite the mating part. She wants something from Ellelin, I can just tell. This is about far more than her husband. Fuck, I don't care at this point. Six months is plenty of time to find Ellelin and make sure she is safe for the rest of her life. I won't force her to be my mate, nor will the others, and I will take whatever the deal demands for not completing it. We took Ellelin from her home, forced her to compete in a deadly test, and she deserves to be free. Fuck my soul.

"And what do you get out of this if we complete the deal?"

She giggles. "Love is my power. I win either way. Love or your soul. Both are magic to me." Aphrodite is fucking me over, and we both know I'm desperate enough to willingly let her. Shit. I remember my father sitting me down as a young boy after I told him I was frightened of water and how it was the most dangerous thing to our court. He told me that no element could ever be as dangerous as love. Love invades our souls and makes us do anything it wishes. In this moment, I know he was right. Ellelin has my soul, and I'd do anything to keep her safe.

"I'm surprised my husband didn't kill you outright, but then again, your people haven't been as easy to conquer as he planned. He believes your love is dead, but she is not. She is in the West with the riders of the West. They have a new ruler, and once he knows who she is, she will be in great danger."

Pride fills my chest that my people haven't been defeated. "My people will not bow to him, and I will find her first."

Aphrodite walks over to me, placing her hand on my shoulder, her red magic burning through the air as her power intensifies. Her touch burns and I know she is marking me, something permanent to remind me of our promise. Six months to save Ellelin. Six months to save my court. The other kings are going to be pissed at me, especially Lysander, but I don't see them getting us out of here. They are as trapped as I am. This way, we have a chance. "Swear to our deal, King Arden of the Fire Court."

"Deal."

CHAPTER 2

ARTEMIS, DAUGHTER OF THE SORCERER AND APHRODITE.

The screams of the Water Court people never seem to stop. They echo all around me, continuously, as I wait in the throne room. There's not much left of the throne room, compared to drawings I used to study years ago. Now, water has eroded so much of it that only small stone pathways lead up to a huge throne built within an arch. Tall windows pour water down the walls in every direction, and I used to think it looked like it's going to flood, but it drains underneath into the sea below, leaving nothing but puddles and small streams everywhere. The water dragons must love this place.

Now, that water is running red with blood, and dead blue dragons line the once peaceful sand beaches of the sea below. Some of the captured Water Court happily gave in and sided with my father without another word, while others did so to protect their families. But they gave my father everything he needed to get past the protection wards. It was sad, almost, how so many of them turned their backs on King Lysander and his family. His mother escaped, but I'm sure my father will catch up with her soon. The dragon kings deserved this fate, so he says. But the people my father is currently slaughtering, they perhaps do not.

I look up to the blue crystal throne, where he sits lounging upon it. His black cloak smothers the throne as he watches more people being dragged in front of him, crying and weeping. For weeks, my father searched the fifth court castle for the crowns, but he couldn't find them. He did find his staff, which has only made him more powerful. It is held tightly in his grip as he looks down at the traitors. These people who are loyal to Lysander and refused to kneel in front of my father until their legs were broken.

"Bow and pledge yourselves to me," my father breathes out. "Then you can live."

A man in the middle holds his head high. "We

bow only to our true ruler, King Lysander. I curse you in the name of the mighty dragon gods—"

In seconds, my father's staff ripples out an orange fog. It pours out of the blood red crystal on the top and smothers the prisoners, choking them to death. There is silence, like the world seems to wait for their deaths, before the sound of their bodies thuds as they hit the wet ground. I sigh, picking up the skirts of my black dress my father insists I wear as I walk down the middle path, enjoying the feel of the water against my feet. The water that isn't soaked in blood.

A familiar feeling hits me hard in my chest when I see the purple cloak of the dead male who cursed my father. Ellelin. I can't get her out of my mind because my friendship with her wasn't real until it was. I was told to get close to Ellelin, to make her my friend, to get her to trust me. The castle hasn't been claimed by her because she doesn't know how to do that, but it still recognised who she was. Anyone that was friends with her was protected by the castle, and I had to use her. The castle needed to trust me too so it would listen to me when I told the castle that my father was Ellelin's friend and needed her help. From then, it was easy to sway the castle into making sure Ellelin saw my father.

But my mother and father neglected to tell me about how dangerous the test was, how they could easily have let me die in it. I glance up at my father. No. He wouldn't have let me die. It can't be true. He knew that I was going to survive. That I'm strong enough to survive on my own. I'm the daughter of two gods, even if I don't have any powers. I blink away the betraying thoughts once again, the confusion settling deep in my soul alongside the feeling of guilt that I can't shake.

I pause, looking behind me as the doors to the throne room open. The doors themselves are beautiful. Water dragons made of cast iron and blue crystal swirled together. My mother shatters them when she walks in with her magic, the red glow like smoke. The red magic only makes her blonde hair glow lighter like the sun, and every freckle on her cheeks looks like tiny stars. She is beautiful in a tragic way, and I know everyone falls at her feet. My mother is slimmer than me, not a curve on her body, and yet she somehow makes every movement seem so much more. It's strange to see her after hearing her in my head for so long from the place she was locked away.

Last night, I helped her get the dragon kings out and made sure the castle let them escape. My father is going to be absolutely furious when he realises they're gone. He thought she wasn't interested in anything to do with the dragon kings and she was happy just looking after me. Apparently, my mother has her own plans. I love her when she is kind to me, and not when she is cruel.

Sometimes I wonder if she is as trapped with my father as I am. She told me once that there were five gods that came through to this world originally. Five gods that made this world better, brought magic into it before my father got jealous and killed two of them. The third god escaped and hasn't been seen since, according to my mother, and Ares married her to link them forever. I once asked if she loved him—she is the goddess of love after all. She never answered me.

My mother smiles softly at me as she walks past, and I can't help but feel this flurry of wanting to go near her, to side with her. She's a goddess of love and attraction. It makes sense that I'd want to be more loyal to her than I have been to my father. My father straightens, using his magic to throw the bodies aside like they're nothing before looking at her. I think he loves her. "Go back to the castle. Don't interfere."

"Why not? It's more fun to interfere," she coos.

His eyes narrow. "Do you want to get back to our old world?" She doesn't answer. "Then don't interfere."

"Who says I want to go back? You assume I don't like it here." She runs her fingers through a waterfall nearby, letting her magic make it sparkle where she touches. Humans on Earth talk about Greek gods a lot, and my mother told me loads about them in my training to become a normal human, enough to pass the test. I always took it to heart a bit too much, so much so that I almost wanted to be Arty to my friends and Artemis to my parents. Maybe I even wanted to be that person, the person I'd been trained to be, that happy person who had friends. But I do have a family, even as complicated as they are now.

I watch these two very powerful Greek gods talk to each other like they aren't extremely powerful. They didn't come from Earth. My father told me once that the world they came from was filled with wolf shifters, mortals, angels, witches, and some dragons, too. Apparently, gods like him were being hunted thousands of years ago, but he didn't tell me why. They had no choice but to leave that world to gain more power somewhere else, and he planned for them to go back. It didn't work out like that. Now they are left like this, unable to do anything. Aphrodite pauses, crossing her arms, and it pulls up her long pink silk gown. I don't look anything like her. I wish I did. She is far prettier every time I see her. I can't believe I'm related to her half the time. "You like war and death. You are the god of it, but I am not. Your sole mission in life is to make war, suffering and pain, but I never agreed to that."

"Are you challenging me, wife?" he growls, fury building in his eyes.

"You've gone too far this time, husband, and you left me out of the fun. I've fixed things," she exclaims. Shit, she is going to tell him everything. "This is our world now. I don't wish to go back, and you shouldn't either. Who knows what they've done with their gods out there? They were being eradicated the last time we left. We came here for peace. It was only you who did not see that. But you, god of war, could never stop. You had to cause trouble, and you had to destroy the people here. It's going to backfire on you."

He scoffs. "I apologise that you're bored, Aphrodite. I don't see how it could backfire. The heir to the fifth court is dead. The queen lies in my dungeon, powerless, alone and broken after seeing her daughter was dying. The dragon kings' descendants are locked in cages above my throne room. Everything—"

"Are they?" she teases with a giggle.

My father doesn't laugh. Mother looks over at me and winks. My father notices her wink, and the way his eyes narrow makes my heart clench in fear. Sweat trickles down the back of my neck to my spine as I start to panic. "This world was just there for the taking. What have you done?"

She smiles. "I set them free. It's about time someone gave them a chance, and you were never going to do that. You are a god, and you should have killed them."

He growls. "You stupid bitch. It doesn't matter, the fifth court is gone—"

"She's not dead," my mother adds in. "You threw her to the West with the dragons. I watched a dragon swoop her up in the air and mark her as his own. You should know why they would have done that. Not a smart move, Ares."

The ground starts to shake as my father gets very angry. I barely manage to stand as he lashes out at his wife, barely missing her with a blast of orange power as she jumps to the side. She blocks him with a shield of red. "I could kill you like I did the others. It would be easier to open the portals between the worlds and take every world as my own with your power."

She sighs. "We both know you won't do that. I know your heart and it is mine." He doesn't answer her. We all know it's true. She walks out of the room, past me, pausing at the door. "Good luck finding them before they figure out how to stop you. I might help if they do."

She disappears, leaving just me and my father. My very angry father. He storms over to me, grabbing me roughly by the neck and lifting me up into the air. I gasp, crying out at the sudden pain as he holds me so tight and lets his magic rip into the skin at my neck, burning me. "You know your mother isn't well. Did you help her?" He shakes me and I struggle to breathe. I can barely hear him over the sound of my heart racing. "Did you help her get those kings out for your old friend? Did you know she was alive?"

"No," I manage to croak out. He throws me hard onto the floor, hard enough that I hear something in my shoulder crack. I scream out in pain, and he simply steps over me as he walks to the broken doors.

"I have dragon kings to go and hunt. Don't do anything else stupid, my daughter. Don't help your mother play games. She is going to get us all killed," he demands. "If I were you, I'd figure out a way to find your old friend and kill her before I find her. If you want to impress me, that is. So far, I'm finding more reasons to kill you than keep you alive. Go and find out where the water queen is hiding."

I still hear the echoes of screams outside the castle as the court of water falls, drowning all of its people under my father's reign. Climbing to my feet, I leave the throne room and head to the dungeons, letting the castle open the doors for me on the way. The castle is not happy with us all being here, but it doesn't matter for long. All the castles of the royals are enchanted in their own way, like they are alive. Maybe they are, and this castle is close to drowning us all. I stroke the wet, cold wall for a moment. I hope my father stops harming the people of this court soon.

The dungeons are dark, damp, and the perfect home for a Water Court prince. Prince Kian kneels in the middle of his cell, his shirt gone, and lashes drip blood into the puddle of water at his knees. I wince at the sight, even when I'm trained better than that. Showing genuine emotion was knocked out of me young. Literally. My ribs and stomach are on fire with every step, and Prince Kian looks up through locks of fire red hair. He is a pretty prince, and he once healed me, but we are on different sides now.

Prince Kian watches me with green eyes that remind me of his brother. The king who would kill me in a heartbeat and is currently missing. "I need to know where your mother is hiding. It's better for her to come out now than let hundreds, if not thousands, die in my father's search."

He ignores my question, or at least he pretends he didn't hear me. His eyes burn like a green jewel. "You're injured. I can sense it. How did that happen?"

Instinctively, I hold my side. "That doesn't matter—"

He lifts his head. "To me it does. You want me to talk, then you talk first, Artemis."

I grab an old wooden chair and drag it in front of the bars. A few cells down is the spirit queen, locked away from view, and for a second, I let myself look. Father brings her to every court, every

19

castle we visit, as he doesn't want to risk her escaping. She is powerless, so he claims, but I doubt it. He wouldn't be keeping her alive and locking her up on his travels if she posed no threat.

There is a secret here, but I don't know what it is. I focus again on the handsome prince. Even when I knew it was impossible to like anyone in the Crown Race, I found myself looking at him.

I've always loved the sea. The sound of the waves. Even the storms and lightning that regularly flashed outside where I grew up. Maybe it's why I stay, just to look at him for a moment longer. "Fine, I sided with my mother over something, and my father didn't like it. I'm used to it though. He has a temper and—"

Anger and sadness flash in the depths of his eyes that I can't look away from. "You don't deserve to be hurt because he has a temper. You don't deserve to be hurt. Period."

I huff. "You don't know what I deserve. I'm not a good person."

He shrugs a shoulder and rises to his feet. Magic symbols have been drawn into his chest by my father, blocking his magic with a powerful spell. I heard his screams and threw up after they were over because I don't like cruelty or pain. I never have.

Taking life was something I was taught to do well, but I had to teach myself how to be a zombie when I do it. No feelings and make sure I forget it quickly. Or I'd crumble from the guilt. I'd be swallowed up by it.

"Doing bad things because you don't know another way does not make your soul bad. You can change and help me. I won't tell you where my mother is and no one in this court will. Not even the ones sided with your father. He does not care for you, Artemis. You never injure those you love."

I kick at a pool of water. "What do you know of it?"

He looks right at me. "I remember a time when my father would hurt me for being weak. He had this game, to test royal sons. My mother never knew, and Lysander…he pretends it was a game and not cruel. The game began by taking us out into the sea and leaving us out there to survive. Storms, snow, heat waves…it didn't matter. If we couldn't survive in the sea on our own for a week, then we weren't true princes of the water. We were forced to wear jewels of old magic that stopped us from shifting or using our powers. I only had to survive twice, but Lysander…it must have been countless times, or more games I never knew of, because he

21

was the heir. Even now, Lysander loves his father and can't see how any of it was wrong. You're the same as him. But you can change."

I try not to feel terrible for him, but I find myself realising we are similar. My father likes to play games, so does my mother. I'm always caught in the middle. "How did you survive?"

Kian snorts, and his smile shows his dimples. Something about his smile makes me smile back. "A whale."

"A whale?" I ask with a bigger smile.

"Yes, it found me and let me live on its back for the week. I was starving and cold, but alive," he explains, almost fondly. "We might have been two creatures from different worlds, but we understood each other. Like us. When my father died, I tried to talk to Lysander about the games and how it wasn't his fault. He just got angry, wanting to avenge our father's death. Our father's death was a gift from the mighty dragon gods for us. He won't see that."

A scream echoes from outside, followed by the echo of my father shouting my name. I didn't get any information that is going to please my father, and in the mood he is in, I know he will beat me for it. My father says punishment is painful so it teaches me a lesson. I never know what the lesson is. I shake my head and stand up, trying not to reveal every inch of my fear across my face for Kian. I feel like he can see right through me, into my dark, crumbled soul. I leave the chair where it was. "I have to go."

"Come back?" Kian asks. "Just to talk. You don't have to tell me anything or help me. No catches."

I find myself nodding once, unable to admit that talking to him might help me survive the games my father is playing. He is my whale.

A soul-stirring song plays over and over in my mind, like it's real and I can taste the music in the warm air. I can't stop the song playing in a loop, like it's calling to me. Like it's begging me to remember something I just can't. The song reminds me of shadows and darkness, and dragons.

"She's waking up."

I hear a soft, melodic voice one more time before the world seems to come back to me. She repeats the same thing, that I'm waking up, but soon I can tell she has left and I'm alone. I can feel heat sticking to my skin, reminding me of my childhood and a heatwave that went on for what seemed like forever. The smell of something sticks to my senses.

It smells like medicine with a sharp herbal tang that makes me feel sick. I need to wake up. I need to get up. Everything is so foggy. I feel like I'm pushing through muddy water to climb to the surface of a lake, only to find its bank covered in a sharp incline of mud. With no one and nothing to help you get out.

When I eventually can open my eyes, I gasp in the warm, sticky air until it fills my lungs. It's so hot here. A light sheen of sweat covers my entire body, and it feels like I'm lying in the sand. I stretch my fingers through the hot grainy matter and frown. Sand? I try to sit up, only for something to push against my chest and legs. I look down at dark blue vines that are thickly wrapped around my entire body. They are heavy, almost holding me down, and as I look closer, I notice they are leaking some kind of clear dust onto me and the sand, which is what smells. I'm wearing a thin, almost see-through white dress.

Grunting, I manage to push enough of the vines to my waist so I can sit up, the room spinning as my violet hair falls over my shoulders and past my waist. I don't remember my hair being that long. A strand falls down near my cheek, too dark to be violet. Black strands fade into light purple. My hair has grown…a lot. The black is down to my chin, and I've grown so much hair.

"How long have I been asleep?" I whisper, barely managing to get the words out. Where the hell am I and what happened? I try to remember, but it's like I just can't. I know I'm in shock and, the moment it wears off and I really wake up from this, it's going to come back to me, and the feeling of dread in my chest is going to be explained. I look around at where I am, trying to connect some of the dots. It's humid, a sticky heat, and a few bugs are flying around the air nearby within the giant tent I'm in.

The tent is moving slightly in the wind, but I can't feel the breeze in here, and it's light out, the dark brown tent hiding most of the sun outside. The tent itself seems to be made of a thick material, and there isn't a hole to be seen. I'm the only one in here, but there are several more raised beds like the one I'm in, filled with yellow sand and blue vines. I pick up more of the vines around my legs, sliding my feet out from under them. "Slow now. The *Craobhteth* tree wrapped around you is alive and doesn't take well to sharp movements while it finishes healing you. It's also worth a small fortune, and damaging it would be costly to you."

I nearly jump out of my skin at the sound of a feminine voice and swiftly turn around to watch as a female walks in from a gap in the tent, bright sunlight surrounding her for a moment, so I can't see anything but how tall she is. When the gap is closed, she walks to me. She is willowy, with light grey hair and tanned skin. Her hair is pulled up out of her face, messily, like she had no time in the morning to do anything but throw it together with a band. Tiny black-framed glasses are perched on the end of her nose, and they are strange, nothing like the glasses on Earth. The lenses are gold, and I don't know how she could possibly see through them. But there's something very human about her as she walks over to me. "Be careful getting out of the healing sand. Let me get some steps for you."

"Where am I?" I manage to say, though my voice is croaky and broken. I don't hear her short reply as she walks to the other end of the tent, because I remember. Everything starts to hit me about where I was, and my heart starts racing faster and faster. The last test of the Dragon Crown Race comes back to me in a flood of memories, so fast I can't think of anything else. The snakes, Florence dead, the sorcerer and Arty. The fifth court...the castle. I'm the princess of the fifth court. The court that was destroyed twelve years ago. My parents were the king and queen of the fifth court, and I was home the entire time I was in the castle.

The sorcerer, the being that made the curse on the dragon kings in the first place, is free. I unlocked him from his cage that my parents put him in somehow. Arty... I still can't believe she's his daughter, and she was playing with me this whole time. It couldn't have been all fake, but she killed the others in the test and used me. Everything she said to me, the times I saved her life, it couldn't have been all fake. If it was, she's the greatest goddamn liar that I've ever known.

The dragon kings are in so much danger. I need to warn them. A gentle breeze blows in from a flap in the tent, fanning my hair around my face, and the dark strands make me realise that the time for that might well and truly be gone. He's probably killed them for all I know. Something deep down in my heart hurts at that horrible thought. In fact, it tears my heart to shreds. No, they can't be dead. I refuse to believe it until I'm sure. They could have escaped, just like Arty said Hope and Livia did. The top of a ladder is shoved roughly against the side of the bed.

"Out you get, child," the woman commands, her voice strict enough to make me move. My entire body feels like I've run the whole stretch of my hometown as I manage to climb out of the bed and down the ladder. My bare feet sink into thick, warm sand as I stand on shaky legs. The woman looks me up and down as she stands in front of me, assessing me in a way that makes me think she is a doctor or healer of some kind. With her hands folded together in front of her, she nods at a small table at the front of the raised bed, right behind me, where there is a jug of water and a glass. "Do help yourself to water, as I'm sure you have questions, and your throat will be dry. It is a side effect of the Craobhteth. Drink slowly so you don't throw it up."

I shakily pick up the glass and begin pouring water into it, missing the glass and soaking my hands as they tremble. She looks like she wants to come over and help me, but she doesn't move; she simply watches me with her grey eyes. As I drink, enjoying the warm water, I notice she's wearing dark brown leathers that cover her from the neck down to her feet where she's wearing long boots. I've never seen anything like what she's wearing. The corset itself is tight around her waist and breasts, and there isn't much skin showing other than her arms, which don't have leather covering them. She must be boiling hot in that.

Once I've drunk half the glass, she relaxes her shoulders. "My name is Healer Ainela of the West Riders' Army, who serve Tsar Aodhan. To answer your question, you're in the West of Ayiolyn, and you are serving the tsar now. This is our war camp, where we collect riders and look after them. We heal them as they choose their dragons, as it can be a dangerous time. We go every five months into the dragons' territory, where we make camp there for two months. They allow us to stay as long as there's riders with them. The next *Taghadh* is in a few days, and you'll be going."

Taghadh? What the hell is that? I have so many questions and I don't know where to begin. "I don't want to be a dragon rider for your war, or the tsar, or any of this. I have—"

Her hands slip to a green dagger I didn't see at her waist. "You serve the tsar, or you are our enemy. Choose wisely your next words, stranger."

I lift my head and grit my teeth. "I feel like I

don't have a choice here." She doesn't reply to that, but it's clear that I'm right. I'm in the West, and once again I'm being thrown into some kind of test I didn't want to enter. Somehow, this one seems worse. I don't know much about the West. No one spoke of it. "So, I'm still in Ayiolyn—"

"Yes. Where else would you be?" She frowns at me, and I realise I didn't mean to say that out loud. "No one knows exactly where you came from, and your accent is very strange."

"So is yours," I comment.

She smiles at that. "I know you're human, or I would have known by now. I've been looking after you for months. A dragon shifter would have healed faster."

"Thank you for looking after me, even if you're now signing me up for a war," I mutter. I'm getting really tired of this shit. I was so close to finishing the Dragon Crown Race and...well, I don't know what would have happened after that, but I know it would be better than this. "I'm definitely human." That feels like a lie even as I say it. Am I human? Half human? I don't even know. I wasn't born on Earth, and my parents... God, what am I? The fifth court. Everything the sorcerer said seems to repeat over in my mind.

"You're from this world. You are the princess of the Spirit Court, the last living heir." He says it with disgust in his tone, and I can't believe him. I don't... but—*"The magic that locked me in here was from your family; therefore, it was only your blood that could get me out. I sent my daughter into the test. I wanted to make sure that she could get close to you, and she did. She told me you even called her your friend. How pathetic and how easily you trust some-one. You're a long way off the great spirit dragon king and queen. They would be ashamed of you."*

Do I have those powers? "Where are you from and what is your name?"

"Ellelin," I begin, crossing my arms. It only just hits me that I'm wearing nothing more than a see-through dress. "Do you know about other worlds?"

She nods. "Yes. Although many of them are lost to us now. There used to be gateways between the worlds, portals and such, but magic like that was taken thousands of years ago and warped by an evil male who was not from this world. We all know the stories. Why?"

"I'm from Earth and I am not meant to be here. I want to go back to the courts—" Her eyes narrow at me. "You're at war with them, aren't you? That was probably a really stupid thing for me to say."

"We are at war with them, child, and it is best you do not mention where you are from to anyone else. I won't kill you, because loyalty to the courts is pointless now. Something is wrong with them," she states. I go to ask what, but she keeps talking. "Don't mention the courts or how you managed to get here. All you need to do is make sure they understand that you have that *comharrachadh* marking on your chest, so you're meant to be here because the dragons will it."

"What mark?" I demand, pulling the dress forward. Right on my chest, right above my breasts, are three long markings that match the black ink on my back. Each of the lines looks like shadows against my skin, stretching all the way up to my shoulders on each side in rows of symbols I've never seen. It looks like a dragon claw, and for a second, I remember the dragon with black scales that swooped down and picked me up after the sorcerer threw me through the portal. Did that dragon do this to me? It's too delicate for a dragon that big to have done it himself, but maybe some kind of magic I don't understand did.

I look up at Healer Ainela, knowing she must have seen the crown on my back and the dragons on my wrists. I glance at them now, seeing four

33

dragons now. The earth test marked me… I did win the test. Not that it means anything now. Healer Ainela follows my gaze. "You might wish to hide those, too. I'm not sure what they are, but others might understand more than I."

"They are just markings," I quickly say. Too quickly.

"In this world, and in others, marks are very rarely just markings," she responds. "You were brought here by a dragon and marked. That is unusual. The wild dragons rarely venture out of their own territories, and markings like yours happen in their territories when you are chosen as a rider. If dragons do find a stray human wandering around in the desert, they're usually a snack. But a dragon saved you and dumped you in camp for me to save. You are unusual, and many have questions you will need to find answers for. For instance, the bite was very strange. It was not a venom I'm used to seeing here. It stopped your heart a couple of times. It took me a while to work out what the bite was before I could heal you." She looks at my hand, where Arden's ring is still on my finger, but the green gem no longer glows. "That magical ring definitely saved your life. Whatever magic was in it, it's gone now. But it did work, along with my help.

You shouldn't have any issues with your broken leg either; that has healed."

I really don't know what to say to all of that. "Thank you for saving my life."

She waves a hand. "The dragon saved your life by marking you. I would have left you to die. You look like trouble, child. The mark means you have great potential to be a dragon rider for our war if the commander decides you are worth the effort. Make sure you understand which side you're on when you speak to the commander. You may be marked, but if you mention that you're loyal to the courts, you'll end up dead. The commander is the tsar's brother."

Great. I have to convince some asshole that I want to fight in a war, which I don't want to fight in, against a people that I want to get back to. It's certainly one way to get back to the courts. If I ever want to see the dragon kings and my grandmother again, I have to get back. I look at her. "Why are you warning me and helping me?"

"You're young and death is a wave on this land. I need not throw you into the wave when I can hold you on land. You haven't tried to run or declared loyalty to the courts," she answers. But I was in a test to become one of their queens. I have feelings for the kings. I'm loyal to them even if I never wanted to be. I don't say any of that. "Come, we should get you changed and to the girls' tent."

"How long have I been asleep?" I demand as she walks to the flap in the tent where she came in. I have to jog as she is so tall and walks too fast. I flinch at the bright sunlight outside as she pulls back the flap and hooks it to the side. She pulls a dark cloak off a hook on a wooden pillar and hands it to me. I quickly clip it over my shoulders, pulling my arms through the sides. "You've been asleep for four months," she tells me. "Four months to cheat death. Lucky girl."

Four months. All I can think about is Arden, Emrys, Grayson and, fuck, even Lysander. Some stupid part of me doesn't want him dead either, not unless I kill him myself. They could all be dead. Actual physical pain seems to slam straight into my chest at the thought of that. I never got to tell Arden how I feel. I never got to reply to Grayson when he told me he wanted me to survive the test for him. Emrys…I wanted more time with him, as every moment was more fun than I've had in years. Lysander…well, he needs to die in front of me, because I don't trust the fucker to somehow cheat his way out of a death that he deserves for being a disloyal, blackmailing, devastatingly attractive bastard.

We step out into the bright sunlight of the desert that surrounds us. The air is dry, and I can almost taste the sand with each breath. People walk past, looking our way briefly, but I block them out. My feet sink into the hot sand, and my eyes widen. There are thousands of tents spread around me like a brown wave against the yellow, nestled within dunes. I look up as two massive green dragons fly above my head, roaring to the sun, followed by several black ones that are smaller. On their backs are riders holding onto them from something like saddles, their brown leather cloaks whipping behind them.

"Fucking hell, this can't be happening. I'm in a war." I whisper it to myself, my heart pounding with each word. I realise that I'm in far more danger than I ever was in the Crown Race.

"Bring the stranger to my tent. NOW!" a man shouts from across the clearing. I can't see him, nothing but the outline of a tall bulky man in the entrance of the tent opposite. The tent is slightly different from the others. The top is red tipped, and dragons made of steel line the edges, like they are holding it up.

The man goes back into the tent, where two guards stand outside. A sinking feeling enters my chest. "Who's that?"

"The commander. You best be very good at lying, child." She shoves her hand in my back, pushing me straight towards the commander's tent.

CHAPTER 4

"*L*eave the stranger with me. You are dismissed."

Ainela raises her voice to the commander. "Of course, *ceannasaí*."

The demand is barked the second we step in front of the tent door and look up at who must be the commander. I won't beg Ainela to stay. I don't trust her either, and she doesn't hesitate before walking away into the crowds and tents. Moments after she has left, another barking demand carries to me. "Come in out of the sun before you burn."

A nervous energy fills my chest as I step into the cool tent. The tent glows red from the sun shining through the thick tarp, and yet, it is somehow much cooler in here. Thick, rich red carpet is spread

39

around the tent, and in the middle of the tent is a large wooden desk with a map spread across it. Mini statues are everywhere on the map, and books line the sides of the tables. I recognise it as a map of Ayiolyn.

Continuing to scan the space, I notice there are sectioned off areas to the sides and back of the room, and sitting behind the desk is a tall, very good-looking man. He's got to be a good five years older than me, at least, with short red hair and dark brown eyes. He watches me quite cautiously with a practiced mask of indifference. When his eyes slowly drift up my body, he meets my eyes. "Come and sit anywhere you wish. What is your name?"

I look at the many seats in front of the desk and cross my arms. "I've been lying down for a long time. I'd prefer to stand."

"Name?" he shouts, clearly annoyed with me.

"Ellelin Ilroth."

He looks me over once more before standing up off his seat and walking around the desk. He isn't wearing leather like the others I've seen, but armour that is layered over black clothes that show off his body. "Fine. We will stand. I'm Commander Ivan. Welcome to the tsar's army." He's taller than me and he holds himself in a way that leads me to suspect he hasn't been around a lot of people taller than him. He's not quite as tall as the dragon kings, but definitely over six foot. He walks around me in a circle, still watching me. I don't like how close he is getting with every loop. "Tell me, Ellelin, where are you from? How did you get here?" He flicks a strand of my purple locks. "Strange hair."

When I don't answer, he moves in front of me. I can't see any weapons on him, but I suspect if he wanted me dead, I'd be dead within seconds. "Fine, let's get to the most important question. Who are you loyal to?"

I know the next words out of my mouth will decide whether or not he kills me. I've met dangerous people before, and he has that look. I have to make my lie good, or as close to the truth as I possibly can get, without him knowing I am from the Dragon Crown Race and close to his enemies. "I'm from the courts." It's not exactly a lie. I was apparently born there and lived there until I was six years old, but he doesn't need to know all the details. "I fell through a portal, and it landed me here in the desert. I didn't choose to go through it and, of course, I was injured." Not a lie. Not exactly. "I find myself here randomly."

"Yes, I'm aware you were found in the desert

and very injured. Most of the healers gave up on you, but you were lucky one didn't," he responds with a disdainful look. He was definitely one of the people willing to let me die. "But you didn't answer my question. Are you loyal to the courts where you were born? To the dragon kings? Or are you loyal to my brother, the tsar?"

"I am not loyal to anyone." Lie. Lie. Lie. Thankfully, I don't blurt out my inner thoughts. "I do not know who to be loyal to. I know nothing about the riders of the West, what they're called in the courts. I was never loyal to the courts, either. I'm finding myself in need of help and somewhere safe, and apparently, I've been marked as one of your dragon riders. So, it's looking like I'm finding myself on the side of the tsar." For now.

He moves closer, too much *closer*, and right into my personal space. I want to take a step back, but I feel like that would show him fear. I need to be strong, or I'm not going to get through this. Right now, I need to convince him that I'm not an enemy so I don't get kicked out in the desert for a dragon to eat me. Lying to survive seems to be my life. I'm not sure how I'm going to get back to Earth, to my grandmother, who must be so, so worried.

I wonder if she thinks I'm dead now, and I

wonder if she knows that I'm in this fricking world she never told me about. I can't believe she didn't know, considering her daughter was a queen. She must know about magic. There's no way she couldn't have. My heart hurts at the thought she lied to me all this time. I want to ask her so many questions, and I want to believe she didn't know. I've already been betrayed by Arty, found out I'm a princess of the Spirit Court, and my family were slaughtered. If my grandmother knew and lied to me...I don't know how to handle that.

He reaches out and touches both my shoulders, spreading his fingers out to brush against my collarbone. His touch is cold, and I really don't like the fact he's touching me. I get the feeling that he's good looking enough that he's used to anyone and everyone bowing at his feet. But that won't be me. "You are loyal to me now. That's all I need to know, and you're safe at my side. You've been marked as a dragon rider, and I'll make sure to keep you close to my side, so you're safe. You won't be going back to the courts anytime soon. Not that anyone can."

I step back from him. He looks like he wants me to thank him for that creepy offer, but all I can hear is his comment on the courts. I try to keep my voice calm. "What does that mean? About the courts?"

Commander Ivan narrows his eyes. "A few months back, magic smothered the courts, and we can't see in or get in at all. We used to be able to invade their shores, take people to be our riders, save families, and liberate them from the hell of the court life they live." I'd like to ask them if they feel saved. "But now their magic smothers their land to protect them. We know they're building an army to attack us. It was only a matter of time before they came after us for attacking them first. My brother knows this, so we are building our army larger than it ever has been before. We are ready for the attack. We will not lose our lands, but we will conquer theirs. Welcome to the war."

"Why attack them at all? Why go to war?" I question, my heart pounding.

He leans against one of the chairs. "Because dragon shifters do not belong in this world. We were here first, and they came, conquered, and destroyed. Their ancestors killed ours when they came to this world and made themselves kings. Magic didn't exist, and there was peace until them. My brother is in complete control of the continent where everyone believes in a world of peace with no magic. We will win because our land and army are five times larger than the courts. We may not have magic, but it does not mean that we are not in a position to rule. My brother united these lands and was the first dragon rider. They were all once wild dragons of the West, and they did not have riders. This land was nothing more than dragons running rampant, killing, and burning mortals. Twelve years ago, my brother went to the dragons and came out a rider. The dragons seemed to decide to let us be their riders permanently after him. More dragons allow riders each year, and they are even picking riders, like you."

"So, you hate magic?" I ask. "But love dragons? Aren't dragons magic?"

"They are creatures of this world; dragon shifters and their magic are not," he states, like it's logical and I should understand. I don't. What did magic ever do to him? "You have your answer, Ellelin. You are mortal and should understand this. You don't know much of our history, not that I'm surprised when you're from the courts. They keep everyone in the dark over there, but you are on the right side now. Find your dragon and train to be a rider with us. Help us take back our world."

I want to say I'm from Earth. So, unless it's history on World War Two, I really don't know anything about it because my school education lacked in areas outside of that. I need a history lesson on Ayiolyn to know what is true and what is not. Either way, he sounds insane to me. Dragon shifters can't help who they were born to be, and hunting them for existing is madness.

"Do not look like that. You are not alone. We have many new female riders. With the new men, that makes two hundred of you. If you're lucky, ten percent of you will make it as riders. If not, you're dead and it doesn't matter which side you're on. I'll take you through to the female tents. We have more riders this turn than ever before, in fact."

He walks past me, putting his arm out, catching my shoulder, slowly drifting his hand down my arm. I pull it away and he smiles. "Being at my side has its bonuses, you know? War is hard for most females, but I'm your friend now. I will make sure you're safe." He opens the tent door. "I think we can get along really well together, don't you?"

Fuck no. I tightly smile to get him to look away from me. There is something so…slimy about him. I can't put my finger on it, but I don't like that he has noticed me at all, and I'm trapped here with him in charge. Outside the tent is a flurry of activity, and I realise that the brown leathers seem to be some sort of uniform that all of them are wearing.

I get many odd looks as we walk past dozens of similar tents, probably because I'm as pale as anything and my hair is purple. All of them are very tanned from the hot sun and desert life. Sand blows into my eyes, and I struggle to cover them up until Commander Ivan reaches over and pulls up my hood. I look up at him. "Thanks."

We stop in front of a long tent, and he opens the door. "This is the women's quarters. I'm not allowed in, regrettably. You can look around, but don't wander far. Leaving the camp without my permission is a death sentence by dragon fire."

With that threat, I step inside the tent, and he looks at me for a second too long before dropping the tent flap. He is a threat on his own. I rub my face before heading down the tent, which stretches on and on. Sleeping areas are tucked into the tent walls, only walls of canvas between them. There are no beds either, just hammocks with netting around them to stop the bugs. As I pass a few, I spot several people inside, all of them giving me very hostile looks. When I get near the end, I pause as a familiar face looks back at me, almost dropping a basket in her arms. "Hope?"

She frowns. "You know, out of all the people

that I could bump into here, it had to be you. I really, really hoped you died back there."

"Who are you talking to like a bitch, Hope? I'm not breaking up another fight because you just had to—" Livia pauses when she sees me. Her eyes widen and she runs to me, crushing me in a hug. I don't think she has ever hugged me before. I'm shocked enough to hold her back. "You're alive too."

Hope watches me with nothing but hostility, leaning against one of the pillars that holds the tents up. "How did you get here? Did you escape the courts, too?"

"No, I didn't escape exactly. But how did you two get here?"

"It's a weird story," Livia whispers, rubbing her chest. "Did you find Florence?"

"Yes, and I'm sorry but she—"

Livia looks away and stops me with a lifted hand. "I suspected…but I thought if you survived, maybe she did."

We all stand in silence. "Can you tell me how you're here?"

Hope rolls her eyes as Livia sobs. "We escaped the earth test after passing it. The portal led us outside the castle, and no one was there. We knew something was wrong as the ground started shaking. The next thing I knew, we were being dragged through a portal again. It literally just appeared underneath us. We're here in the middle of the desert in the next moment. I swear I saw Arty standing above the portal before it closed, but that's—"

"Likely real. She's a traitor and betrayed us all," I snap. "She killed everyone else in the test. She slit their throats. I don't know why she left you two alive, but she's a betrayer. She unleashed the sorcerer and—"

"Keep your voice down," Hope whisper-shouts at me before dragging me into one of the sectioned-off rooms, pulling the cloth shut. "Arty did what?"

I explain everything that happened, leaving out the part about the Spirit Court and who I am. I'm not ready to talk about that yet. Hope leans forward. "Lysander. When'd you last see him? I told you not to trust Arty. No one is that nice and clueless."

Of course she would be worried about him and brag about apparently knowing Arty was dodgy the whole time. "The same time that you saw him. I saw Grayson last, but I was dragged under into the test with you."

Hope claps her hands and steps closer with

nothing but fury in her eyes. "You know nothing useful, except that you let out the sorcerer with your bestie and maybe got Lysander and the others killed?" She huffs. "We're trapped here to become dragon riders with the barbaric assholes, which most of us will not survive. Especially not you, as we have been training for months and you've been sleeping like a fucking princess. It's just like the old times. Another test and oh, look, you're the special one again. What a surprise."

"How have you survived all these years being nothing but a total bitch?" I shout at her, annoyed at how close to the truth she is. "I didn't ask for any of this! Don't pretend you're angry at me to hide the fact you're scared about Lysander, and you don't have anyone better to blame than me."

Livia steps in the middle of us before Hope can lunge at me.

A bell rings in the distance, and she shuts her mouth before saying anything else. Livia looks right at me. "The bell marks the camp moving. The commander must have moved the date forward, and you both need to stop arguing over a guy who might not even be alive anymore. We three are alive and in danger, so grow up and cut the shit. We have to claim our dragons next."

CHAPTER 5

The creaky old cart rumbles as it goes over the sand dunes, and every bump makes me nearly fall off the small bench. A sandstorm blows fast around us, blocking the view of anything for so long that I wonder if the soldier driving the cart has a clue where he is going. Sometimes we go fast down the other side of a dune, fast enough to take the breath out of my lungs right before I fall off the seat with the others. This wasn't built to keep us comfortable, but we have been given water and stale wraps with spicy cheese that the heat has melted.

I cover my face more with the soft silk hood that I was given in the camp, huddling further into the bench. I've never been a fan of tropical places, I don't even like saunas, and this desert is awful. It only gets worse as the hours go on. I look across at Livia, who is sitting straight, watching the desert pass by. Hope is at her side, and she leans in to whisper something to her. They seem to have gotten close in the months that I was sleeping. They didn't speak to me much after the bell went off, because everything was hectic after that point. I'm glad to have found them here, but all I can think of is escaping and the truth I've learnt.

I'm itching to ask Hope what she knows about the Spirit Court, but I know she would want to know why I'm interested, and I can't say it out loud yet. Speaking about it means it's true, and I'm happy to live in my denial house I made for myself. Princess? I never wanted to be one. I was the kid who dressed up as a zombie for World Book Day, while all the other girls were in princess dresses.

The cart bumps and I clutch the seat to hold on. After the commander rang the bell, it was only two, maybe three, hours later before the entire camp was packed up, ready to go, and we were moving out. I look over at the dozens of carts pulled by camels that drag us across the desert, never stopping, never pausing. At the front, I can see the commander in the distance, and I glance down at the other women who are in the cart. There are ten of us in here, and none of them has said a word to me. Not that I blame them. I'm new and they likely think I'm going to get myself killed soon. I mean, it's likely true. I somehow survived the Dragon Crown Race by the skin of my teeth, and I doubt that is happening again.

Hope meets my eyes only for a second to glare at me before looking away. Even she seems nervous, nervous enough not to start a fight with me for the last few hours. If Hope is nervous, we are all screwed. One of the girls down on the end is crying hysterically, and everyone has moved away from her. I rub my face before moving down the cart and sitting next to her. "I'm Ellelin. What's your name?"

She looks up at me through her dark brown hair. Her eyes match the colour of her hair, and freckles cover nearly all of her dark-skinned face. "C-Cordelia."

I lean my head back, keeping my voice soft. I'm not judging her, but I don't know how to help her exactly. "Why are you crying?"

She has stopped crying at least. Cordelia rubs her cheeks that have gone red. "It's stupid to cry, I know that, but with the mighty dragons cursing me—"

"Mighty dragon gods? I've heard of them where I came from," I interrupt her. Part of me wants to know more, but mostly I want to distract her so she stops crying. "They represent the elements, right? Do people here worship them?"

Cordelia nods, sitting up straighter. I smile to myself as my plan to distract her seems to be working and she continues. "Yes, some of us have the same gods as the court lands, but others forsake them. It is known that the five gods came to this world and bred magic and dragon shifters. Here, most people treat the gods like a curse and hate them. My parents came from the courts, and they taught me that the gods cannot be blamed for everything that happens."

"Sounds like most religions." I smile tightly at her. "The Twilight, I think that's what they were called. People tend to worship them in the courts."

She nods. "I've heard of them. They aren't welcome here. Maybe if they were, I wouldn't be going to my death now."

I bump her shoulder into mine. "You might not die. You might find a dragon and soar through the skies." I lower my voice. "Flying a dragon is incredible. Trust me."

"Yeah, trust her. Fucking dragons, even if they

are someone else's boyfriend, is a hobby of hers," Hope snarls, clearly listening in. The other girls all laugh, and Livia shakes her head.

Cordelia looks at me with wide eyes. "You seem too nice to do that."

"I haven't touched her boyfriend." I make sure my voice is loud enough that Hope hears. She doesn't respond, but that isn't a surprise to me. "It's going to be a long trip, so no more crying. If you want someone to talk to, I'm here."

Cordelia smiles for the first time, the sun shining off the silver bracelets that are a contrast to her dark skin. "Thank you."

We don't leave the cart, except for occasionally being allowed to go for the toilet in the sand. We only have privacy by the other girls holding blankets up for us so we can pee in the sand one by one. It's not dignified, but it's better than the rest of the army watching. I'm just thankful I haven't had my period as I'm not on the tonic from the castle anymore.

The sun is setting, casting a red-hot glow across the desert, when the cart suddenly stops. I glance forward, and I don't see anything other than endless sand dunes that are mostly hidden in the lingering sandstorm. I don't see any dragons either. "How is this the dragons' home? There isn't a dragon around."

Livia leans forward. "I heard that the dragons have an underground cave system that is literally under the desert itself. Massive, spiralling caverns. That's where the dragons live. They don't have to fly above land very often. It's too hot for them out here. I guess they made their own home where it's cooler and safer to keep their dragon eggs until they hatch."

I rub my face as I lean back. An underground cave system sounds difficult to escape from. I'm not sure where I'd go, anyway. I'm not safe anywhere, but I'm tired of being the victim. I'm tired of being the kidnapped pawn forced into deadly situations. My hand falls on my chest where the new marks are, and I feel a strong burning throughout my veins. It's gone as quickly as I feel it, and I frown as I pull my hand away. What was that? Maybe it was a link to the dragon that marked me? I don't remember much about it; I was nearly knocked out when it swooped me up out of the sand with its claws. I remember its black scales and green eyes. I have to hope that the dragon doesn't want me dead when I try to become its rider. It found me in the desert and obviously brought me to someone who could save my life, but if it's wild, I can't assume it won't kill me.

"Out you get and take one each." I jump, barely noticing the soldier at the end of the cart. The burly man opens up the cart for us, and I'm at the end now that I've moved next to Cordelia.

I climb off first, and a small tonic bottle of something red is shoved into my chest. "What is it?"

"It will make you infertile for three years and stop your menstrual cycle. The dragons can smell blood and might attack you. It's happened in the past and we learnt from it. As for pregnancies, no rider needs that worry and everyone fucks to relieve tension," he explains, loud enough for all the girls to hear. I happily down the tonic that tastes sweet before handing him the empty bottle back. I don't plan on fucking anyone, but I'd rather not be eaten by a dragon when Aunt Flow turns up.

The soldier watches each of the girls take the tonic, and when everyone is off, he waves a hand in the direction of the front of the army. Other groups, who I assume are new riders, follow alongside us. Slowly, I spot the commander at the front of the carts and camels, on his own, watching something I can't see. The commander looks back straight at me, and I turn away.

Hope rolls her eyes at me, from where she is walking to my side. I've lost track of Cordelia, but Livia is at Hope's side. "What a surprise. You attracted male attention already," Hope huffs.

I blow out a breath, resisting the urge to just punch her. "Fuck off, Hope."

Livia moves between us again, muttering under her breath about how we both need to change the record or just kill each other already. We follow the soldier right up to the commander, where the entire army has stopped. Then I see it. The sand hides it well, but there's a massive circular opening. Red rocks spiral around in a circle all the way down into endless darkness. But the more I look, the more I can see a bright light below and hear the sound of running water. The edges of the rock walls hold hastily built wooden panel steps in a slope that spirals all the way down, and someone has clipped a rope to the wall next to it. It doesn't look very secure.

"The dragons' territory is below, and you will either come out with a dragon or you don't come back," the commander begins, raising his voice. "There are some rules, so listen up. Dragons are welcoming you as their guests, and they speak to their riders. Anyone down there is blood bound to a dragon, but you are not their friend. Do not try talking to other dragons. They can't understand you and they will kill you for a misunderstanding. The dragons' eggs are precious to them, and if you go anywhere near one, death would be kind compared to what the dragons will do to you. The same goes for their young, but you won't see them often. There are parts of the dragon territory we are not shown. At the bottom of the path is your first test, made by the dragons. There are four pathways. One of them will call to your soul, and that will be your chosen path for your dragon. Gold or silver. Let the dragons guide you." With that death pep talk, he waves a hand at the beginning of the path. "Go down and don't fall off. The dragons don't like human splattered across their home."

I take a step forward, only for the commander to walk straight to me. "Not you."

Frowning, I cross my arms. "Why not?"

"Playing favourites, commander?" Hope sarcastically questions from my side. I swear she stepped closer when he came to me.

Commander Ivan barely even looks at her, which goes down well when Hope looks like she is ready to burst. "There is no point in Ellelin going down there when she is already marked by her dragon. The rest of you need to be chosen. She does not."

"That isn't fair!" Hope shouts at us both. "She—"

"Who are you to question me?" he shouts back at her, and she pauses. Not with fear, but I think she just remembered she doesn't have Lysander's protection here. Hope was brought up as a ward of the dragons and protected as such. I guess running her mouth is a bad habit she got into because no one ever told her to shut up. Who would dare when she was a ward of a dragon queen and likely going to become one herself? "Ellelin will be with me, on my dragon, and she will be fine. Go, before I punish you for questioning me."

Livia is waiting for her near the steps, and some other girl is trying to convince Cordelia to move when she is crying again. Hope doesn't move, her eyes flickering to me. "I'll catch up with you down there."

Hope looks at me one more time before leaving with Livia and Cordelia. Commander Ivan looks at them go. "So, you know those two? I should have guessed when they appeared randomly in the desert like you, but not as injured."

I nod. "They are from the courts. We met there."

The commander looks down at me, raising an eyebrow. Shit. I realise that I might just have told him a little too much about them and they might have lied when they got here. "I gathered that those two lied to me when they told me they weren't from the courts, but I could smell the magic on them, and they looked different. They have similar markings all over them, like you do, and doesn't take a genius to put two and two together. I only care about their loyalty as dragon riders. We have many riders from the courts."

I jog to keep up with him after he suddenly walks away. When I get to his side, he looks down at me. "Have you been on a dragon before in the courts? No, I doubt it. It can be quite terrifying, but I'll be there for you."

"I'll be fine," I say quietly. I don't want to tell him that, yes, I definitely rode dragons before. Yes, it is always absolutely terrifying, but being on the back of a dragon was the most alive I've ever felt in my life.

He gives me a look that suggests he thinks he

needs to be a hero. One I don't want or need. "You can hold on to me."

I'd rather fall off than hold on to him, but I don't say it. I don't know what he wants, but I really don't like his attention, and I wish it was anywhere else. He grins at me when I simply smile in response. I follow him straight over another dune, which I have to crawl up on my hands and feet by the end. I hear the dragons first, the deep roars and growls that echo through the air and in my ear. Seconds later, I finally see them. They aren't hard to miss. The dragons are spectacular.

There's another entrance to the caves below, and all around the edge of the massive opening are drag-ons, some with riders on their back. I watch as one gold dragon jumps into the opening and flies down so fast I almost miss it. My stomach drops. I'm not doing that. Fuck no. This must be the entrance for them, and I don't see any other way down. "There's another reason I kept you with me. My brother is here. I'd like you to meet him."

"The tsar's here?" The commander nods, offering me his hand to balance me over a dip in the sand. I climb out on my own and ignore his hand. "Why do you want me to meet him?"

He pauses. "Because you're interesting and

you're beautiful. My brother always seems happier when there's a pretty girl around." I frown at him, and he laughs. "I'm joking, of course."

I really don't think he is joking. I'm going to be the pretty distraction, and that's more insulting than anything else he's said to me so far. He leads me straight towards a black dragon. In fact, the only black dragon in a swarm of silver and gold. The other dragons' scales are glittering in the bright sun, but this one, it fits in with the shadows at his feet better. "The gold dragons breathe fire, and they are very swift in the air. The silver dragons breathe pure ice, and when they land on the ground, they seem to have some control over it."

"And black dragons?" I ask.

He stares at the black dragon we are coming to. "There's very few like mine. Not many are bonded to the shadow dragons like we are."

"Shadow dragons. Why do you call them that?" I ask.

"Because that's what they control. Shadows. They're deadlier than any other dragons, and you are marked by one," he informs me. "If you manage to become a dragon rider, you'll be the third one to have ever chosen a shadow dragon in our history."

"Who's the other?

He smirks at me. "My brother." The dragon swiftly turns its huge head our way, roaring deeply at us both. Fear laces up my spine as I look into its bottomless night-coloured eyes. Its mouth is full of rows of sharp black teeth. Dark grey thorns are spread down its back onto a tail that is the shape of a star at the end, full of deadly thorns, too. His dragon reminds me of Arden's in shape and colouring, but there are no signs of fire touching the black scales. He or she is a lot smaller than Arden's, too. In fact, all these dragons are smaller than the dragon shifters. The dragon leans down when we get close and looks right at me, its nostrils flaring.

"Scathitine, my beautiful girl," he introduces us. "This is my new friend, and she must travel with me down. She is marked by your brother."

Her brother? Scathitine is still staring right at me. "What are the chances of her killing me?"

He shrugs. "Some dragons don't usually like guests other than their riders, but you are no usual rider. They don't attack riders of family members, as far as we have seen."

"I'd rather take the planks," I mutter.

"You won't and she says she will take you with us," he states, grabbing my arm and shoving me roughly towards the dragon, making it clear that I'm not escaping this. I glare at him before beginning to climb up the dragon's wing, which is covered in scales that make it easy to climb. He climbs after me, and when I slip a little, his hand goes straight to my ass and pushes me up. I want to tell him to piss off, but this is his dragon, and I'm on the back of it, so I bite my tongue once again. He was just trying to help me.

I climb up and sit between the thorns, like I've done before, wrapping my arms around one and holding on tight. He climbs up next, sitting right behind me. He could have easily sat in front of me, but he leans forward, wrapping his arms around my waist as well as the thorn at my back. His hand spreads across my stomach, and all I feel is repulsed at his touch.

I clamp down tight on my teeth as the dragon jumps swiftly into the air, and all thoughts of him holding onto me are lost as I scream as my hood falls away, my hair whipping around me. The dragon drops straight down into the tunnel, its wings tucked deep into its side, and I struggle to stay on as I clench my thighs. It dives and dives until I feel I can't breathe. It feels like the air is brutally ripping the skin off my body until suddenly light blasts into my eyes, and the dragon stretches its beautiful long wings out, soaring over the cavern.

The land below me is rivers of red, all around a tree made of stone. Rivers of dark red water stretch all the way around a deep, gigantic cavern, cascading in waterfalls in several places that echo. It looks like a giant sphere with branches spread across it in many directions. There is little greenery down here, but instead, red-leaved bushes sprout across the stone branches. It's like someone grew a tree down here and then turned it into stone.

The dragon swoops down past so many of the dragons who are leaning on these ridges. There are massive archways that lead up to tunnels, and she jumps through one of them that has water running through every inch of the walls. We pass through several more tunnels before she turns around and makes a landing. I blink a few times, feeling the cold air blowing around me, so different from the heat above. Nestled in the walls is a campsite with wooden gates, hiding most of my view of the inside. I can just about see the top of tents and smoke rising into the air.

A dragon roar makes me swiftly turn around, looking right across the cavern to the other side, where it's so dark that I can't see anything. The markings on my chest seem to tingle as I stare into the shadows until I gasp, snapping out of it as the commander shakes my shoulder. "Want some help getting down?"

"No," I bite out, still looking into the shadows. I climb off his dragon on my own, basically falling and rolling off her wing, before standing up. Dignified, no, but I'd still rather climb down myself.

Commander Ivan steps closer to me, and I frown at him. He really doesn't understand personal space. "I wouldn't talk to my brother about your true background. Hide those marks or you'll end up dead."

CHAPTER 6

*T*he commander speaks to the guards outside the wooden fenced wall as I watch everything else behind me. The dragons fly around in formations, almost like a dance that they know. The glittering silver and gold dragons seem to move with each other, even with riders on their backs. Other stray dragons are perched on the stone branches, drinking water or napping. They are beautiful, terrifying creatures, but something else about them makes me not want to look away. "Ellelin, come!"

I jump, so lost in staring at the dragons that I didn't hear him the first time. Turning, I follow the commander through the open gates, and the guards shut the gates behind me. There are a series of tents, no more than about twenty, set up in a green area at the front of the opening to the tunnel cavern. There's a river nearby that I spot through the tents, and we pass many campfires that have riders huddled around them. The sound of water and laughter of the people here are drowned out by the echoes of the dragons' roars in the distance.

Commander Ivan leads me deep into the cave, where the tents eventually lead to combat training areas where people are beating the crap out of each other. I'm suddenly thankful for the competition I had against Hope in training and Grayson's training, or I'd be beaten to death in one of these sessions. Some riders stop and look at me as we pass, but not for long, as someone barks at them to carry on. At the end of the training area is a heavily guarded tent that is huge and red. Something prickles across my skin as we get closer to the tent. This tent is similar to the commander's. Silver dragon statues hold up the red flaps of the tent. Ten heavily equipped guards step aside when they see the commander and me come to the entrance.

I stop.

The world stops.

Arden, Grayson, Emrys and Lysander are standing at the back of the tent. Arden's long hair is tied back at his neck, and he is wearing all black, like the rest of them. The king of the Fire Court is like a fire itself, alluring and deadly to look at for too long. His toned, thick body strains the fabric of his shirt and trousers, almost like they could rip at any moment. I may, or *may not*, be hoping for that. Lysander's red hair is cut short, which only makes his devastatingly handsome face and body more defined. Emrys's hair is longer, his white locks falling into his eyes and his gold skin glowing in the light. Grayson...oh Gray. A loose, long-sleeved black shirt matches his tighter black trousers, and a glitter of silver flashes at me from his side. He looks even more muscular, like he has worked out every day since we have been apart.

It's been months, and they are even more impressive to look at. I want them, I realise with a shock, more than I've wanted anyone in my life. They are four gods in my eyes, handsome and beautiful in a way that should be illegal for men to be. They already have so much power; making them pretty to look at just gives them more power. Damn, I'm sure I look like a gaping fish as I do nothing but eye them up and down and eat up every inch of them. Except Lysander—he is pretty, but he is a dick. I ignore the tiny voice in the back of my mind that calls me a liar. Arden's eyes light up when he sees me, and he is across the tent within seconds, swooping me up into his arms. "Princess, fuck, I missed you."

I bury my head in his shoulder, wrapping my arms around his neck. I missed him, too. I breathe in his scent like a drug, letting myself relax for the first time. I don't know when he became my home, when I knew I wanted to be with him, but that's how it feels now.

Commander Ivan touches my shoulder after a second. Lifting my head, I first notice Lysander's wild sea green eyes fall straight to the commander's hand right before he meets my gaze.

Arden turns to Commander Ivan. I swear his entire body burns under my touch. "Take your hand off her or you're dead. No one touches Ellelin."

Commander Ivan slowly takes his hand off me. "Who the fuck are you to threaten me?"

"Brother," a stranger firmly, but gently, calls. "These are the dragon kings of the courts. I'm not sure who the female is, but leave her and come here."

The commander's eyes widen before he turns to his brother. "Have you lost your fucking mind? Why are they here and not dead?"

Arden is done with the commander, and he cups my cheek, turning me to him and then he's kissing me. I gasp at the sudden kiss, and he takes the moment to deepen the kiss, setting my body alight. The rest of the world fades away as he kisses me with so much passion, and I reply with just the same. The ground shakes under our feet, grabbing our attention, and Arden slowly pulls away. "Have something to say, Gray?"

Grayson growls as my cheeks burn, and Arden turns to face him. For a moment, I'm actually worried they are going to fight, with their powers, before Emrys steps up between them. "Enough. We have bigger problems." Emrys turns to me. "Are you okay? Rather than kissing you, Arden should have begun with that."

"Shit, yeah, you good?" Arden questions.

Lysander joins us. "She's fine."

I glare at him. There are so many things I want to ask them, and I don't know where to begin. "I can answer for myself, but yes, I'm okay. How are you here?"

Lysander crosses his thick arms. "You ask your questions later. Now we've had this lovely reuniting, can we get on with this?" His eyes meet mine and I swiftly look away.

The commander's brother, the tsar, walks over to us after speaking quietly to his brother. The tsar is taller than the commander, by quite a bit, and he has dark blond hair that is braided into plaits that fall down his back. He is well built, and his black armour covers his chest over dark clothes. The tsar's light blue eyes find mine. "Ellelin, your friends have been looking for you. How fortunate you walked straight to us."

Arden makes sure that I'm situated straight between him and Grayson, who seems to agree on keeping me here. I look up at Grayson, at how close he is, how I could just reach out and touch his hand. I'm surprised when his rough hand slides into mine, and he links our fingers. I think that's the first time he has ever held my hand first. My heart pounds, knowing how much of a big step that was for him. I still remember what he said to me right before I went into the earth test. Did he mean it? Does he want me as much as I want him? What would that mean for Arden and me? I can't have them both, and I don't want to hurt either of them. God, we have a lot to talk about, but right now we're in a room full of our enemies.

"We always find each other," Grayson answers. "And what my brother claimed is true. Anyone

73

harms Ellelin, they die. Anyone insults her, they die. I'd make sure that fact is well known around your people if I were you, Tsar Aodhan."

My skin flushes as everyone in the room looks at me. Commander Ivan is the first to snap, and he loses it. "Why the fuck would you make an alliance with them? They are insane and use magic! They are everything we have fought against. Have you lost your mind?"

Tsar Aodhan places his hand on his brother's upper arm. "You will understand the truth of everything if you hear me out." After a while, the commander nods, but he looks frustrated. "The sorcerer is back in our world and set on destroying it all. I've seen proof. The sorcerer brought the magic into the world. Magic was dangerous, and in the past, we all worked together to stop him. We need to stop him, or this war is pointless. When we are alone, I will explain the fine details, but for now, we're raising an army to attack the courts and the sorcerer in order to stop him. We will only harm the people there who have sided with the sorcerer. His reign has to end. There's no point me killing the kings when they are good fighters, and they can convince people in the courts to side with us. When the sorcerer is beaten, we have an alliance planned."

"The sorcerer is nothing more than an old fairy tale! They are tricking you—"

"Brother, he is real. Unless we want to spend the rest of our lives in his service or dead, this is the only way forward. Our people will be slaughtered if we don't stop him. I have a mate and daughter to think of," he quietly says.

The commander still isn't pleased. "After we win your war, do you go back into your courts, lock your doors up again, and attack our people with your magic?"

Emrys shakes his head. "We have never attacked your people with our magic. We have only defended ourselves."

Arden growls. "It seems to be you that were attacking our shores and stealing our people. Where are they?"

"Those who survived are riders," the tsar answers. "We need riders for our army, and people from the court are accepted better than our people."

Arden looks down at me. "We'll take you to our court to keep you safe when we take it. Until then, we have somewhere we can go that is safe."

"Ellelin isn't leaving," Commander Ivan states.

All four of the dragon kings turn on him. I'd be absolutely fucking terrified if they all looked at me like that, but he is either too stupid to care or just plain ignorant. "She's marked by one of the dragons. If she leaves without trying to claim him, the mark will kill her. Once marked, you have a year to claim your dragon or die. Old magic makes these rules."

"Fuck off, you just want to keep her here!" Arden disagrees, and actual flames flicker out of his hands. They touch my hand but don't burn me.

Lysander's voice is like ice. "You better not be fucking lying to us."

"My brother speaks the truth. She has been marked," Tsar Aodhan states.

"How long does the test take?" Emrys coolly questions.

"A couple of months during which she will need to learn to ride her dragon and secure her bond so she isn't rejected," Commander Ivan states. "Until then, she belongs to the riders."

Arden growls and looks at the other kings. They do that silent chat thing they seem to do where they can talk without words. I imagine it's just something they have developed over time. "Fine, but we are staying with her. She will sleep in our tent and join you in the morning."

Commander Ivan huffs. "That is against our rules—"

The tsar pats his brother's back. "I'm sure that rule can be ignored this once."

Lysander, Emrys and Grayson walk to the entrance, and Arden wraps his arm around my waist, my skin burning where he touches. The second we are outside of the tent, Arden leans down, his lips brushing the tip of my ear. "When were you going to tell me that you're the heir of the fifth court, princess?"

CHAPTER 7

*N*o one says anything even when there are a million unspoken words between us all. I glance back at the tsar's tent, seeing the commander watching me walk away between the dragon kings, who he hates. He doesn't seem like the type to accept any of this without a fight. The guys lead me to a large blue tent hidden away within the wall of the cave, actually it's pitched against the wall itself. There are no guards outside, and the minute that I go through at Arden's side, Grayson closes the tent behind us. The dragon kings look between each other, a silent conversation, and I take a moment to look around. There's a fire burning in the middle of the room, and the smoke leads to a gap in the tent where it blows out. There are several floor cushions all laid around the fire, on the carpeted floor, and there is one massive bed pressed against the stone wall at the back of the room.

"You're safe here, Ellelin," Emrys informs me, but I don't believe that for one second. Safe? After everything that happened, I doubt it very much.

"When did you get here?" I question, removing myself from Arden's side so I can think straight. Mostly. Being around all of them makes me dizzy at times. I need answers. "How did you find me?"

They look at each other again. Arden looks at me first. "We only arrived last night, and we suspected you were here. Lysander actually—"

"We're here. Nothing else matters," Lysander cuts him off. I glare at him, and he glares right back until I look away, tired of his shit. Arden is frowning at me, and I want to ask how he knows I'm the Spirit Court princess.

"Why don't we sit down?" Emrys questions. "Before Ellelin and Lysander murder each other."

They sit down on the floor cushions, and Gray meets my eyes for a second before looking away. My heart clenches. I know I upset him by kissing Arden, and I'm not sure how to fix it. Arden offers a space next to him, but I don't take it. "No, I'd rather stand."

Grayson speaks first, surprising us all. "What happened to you in the earth test? Start there."

I don't know why *I'm* beginning. I blow out a breath. "It's complicated. In the earth test, it was all horrible as expected with the snakes, but then the castle kept bringing me to the prisons. I'd been there before—"

"When?" Lysander snaps. "You never thought to tell any of us about the castle taking you to some prisons?"

I turn on him with a sneer. "Really? I should have come running to you, Lysander? We got along so fucking well that you're right. It was clearly insane of me not to tell you every secret of mine."

"Ly," Arden gently warns, but his tone is firm. "Let her finish what she was saying. We all kept our secrets."

Lysander huffs, but he doesn't say another word and I carry on. "In the prisons was a woman asking for help, and I never did what she asked. I asked the castle to stop taking me to her. It turns out that the woman was actually the sorcerer in disguise, and I think she took the form of a woman to make me like her more, trust her more. She kept asking me to put

COURT OF DRAGONS AND VOWS

my blood on the cage and on the bars to set her free. Of course I refused. She was just a nutcase." I close my eyes for a brief second. "But in the earth test, I noticed that a girl had her throat slit. They were dead, not from the snakes or the test. I was bitten and injured, and then I suddenly fell through the floor straight into the prison again. Arty was there."

Grayson frowns at me. "The blonde-haired girl that talked a lot?"

I nod, my heart hurting. I let her in, trusted her, and I was stupid to do so. "She took some of my blood and she touched the bars with it. The prison opened, and it was the sorcerer. It turns out my blood was locking him in there and had done for twelve years."

"He told you that you're the heir to the Spirit Court," Arden finishes. Lysander, Emrys and Grayson are nothing short of shocked silent. "I suspected as much. When the sorcerer was freed, the castle locked us in and began playing a song. I remember it from when I was a little kid, and the pieces clicked for me. I remember you."

"You met me? You knew my parents?" I ask quietly, my eyes widening.

His eyes are full of the same sadness I feel every time I think of them. We both lost everything twelve years ago. His parents and mine. "Yes. My parents and others died twelve years ago helping the Spirit Court. I told you once they died with my little brother in an accident, well, that wasn't the whole truth. The accident was the day the Spirit Court fell. My mother and little brother were in your parents' court, visiting. I was asked to go with them, but I didn't. I remember seeing my father leave, and none of them ever came back. I was seven."

"My father went to help." Lysander's voice is cold. "At the call of the Fire Court king to save his wife and child, and what was left of the court."

"So did my father. He got the message too," Emrys adds in. There is so much sorrow in his voice. Four words, but I feel the pain in them. For Lysander, he is so cold and angry, but Emrys lets his emotions fill the air between us.

Lastly, I face Grayson. "My mother went and never returned. My father was…sick or he would have joined them."

Lysander looks at me with nothing but hate. "Your parents led ours to the slaughter."

"They died too," I softly remind him. Silence rings out between us. "And it was all for nothing because the sorcerer is free. He is going to kill us all."

Arden's voice quickens my soul into a burning flame. "I will never allow anyone to ever hurt you again, princess."

Grayson looks right into my eyes, into the fire burning throughout me. "The earth will fall before he touches you. We came to find you and we will protect you."

"We failed once," Emrys speaks next. A stray breeze blows through my hair. "But any storm that comes our way, we are in this together."

Lysander stays quiet, but I didn't expect him to be here, let alone promise to keep me safe. The others briefly glance at him, and whatever is in their expressions makes Lysander look even more pissed off. I clear my throat, returning my gaze to Arden. "When did you first meet me?"

"My mother was her friend," he softly explains. "Your mother came once with you to the Fire Court, and I remember you because you smelt so different from anyone I'd met before. Like ruby red roses, shadows, and jasmine-tipped darkness. She had a strange scent too, but not like yours. She reminded me of the darkness of the night though. You were shy, and that was new to me. Everyone in the Fire Court is fiery, loud, and they speak their mind, but you did not. You hid behind your mother for a long time, and she encouraged you to talk to me." He pauses. "Do you not remember any of this?"

I shake my head. "No. I don't remember being in the courts. I don't remember anything before my grandmother."

"Strange," Arden murmurs. "You had gorgeous long shiny black hair and bright eyes. I knew you looked so familiar to me. I could never put my finger on why. But when the earth test ended and the song played...I remembered you. We danced to that song before."

My shoulders drop and I feel a little of my defences dropping as he continues. "Your mother played that song for us on the piano, and my mum made us dance to it. I didn't want to dance with you at the time, and neither did you. Still, we danced, and I loved the song. It made you smile." He looks at Emrys. "Emrys was telling me about the song and how it was said to be more than just music. That there was power in the song that only the royals of the fifth court can touch. I remember it; I can play it for you when I find an instrument."

"Do you know what happened to the court's people?" Emrys questions me. "There were thousands of people living on that island, in the Spirit

Court, a good seven thousand of your people, and they vanished. Do you remember anything?"

I shake my head. Grayson rubs his chin. "The Spirit Court was not like ours. Their power was extraordinary, and it's hard to believe that many people were killed with no trace. Your father and your mother only let certain people into the court because having that power came with responsibilities. You have power over life, death, shadows, and darkness. You won't shift into a dragon because your kind didn't need them." He stands, coming closer. "I saw your father once. I've seen the spirit dragon he once rode as he left my home after visiting my father. Your power will be incredible if you're like him."

"I don't have any of these powers, and I can't remember. How is this possible?"

"You're the princess of the Spirit Court, and the power must belong to you. But your scent is different from when we met as children, and I don't scent any magic on you," Arden answers me but without any real answer to the mystery.

"I've always thought there was something slightly odd about her scent." Grayson moves closer, breathing me in. "Maybe there's some sort of magic blocking her, stopping her from accessing her full powers and stopping the sorcerer from finding her. The king and queen of the Spirit Court got her out, safe, before the court fell. Maybe they protected her in more than one way."

Lysander crosses his thick arms. "She was brought up on Earth. It makes sense that protections were wrapped around her so she didn't accidentally drown her class in shadows when she was having a tantrum."

He is right. Maybe my grandmother knows what happened to me. Grayson agrees. "We will need to find a way to break the magic, but there is little information on the Spirit Court and how their magic worked. I will train with Ellelin and work out if my magic can sense anything locking hers."

Emrys's eyes meet mine. Sometimes he is so handsome that it makes me forget to breathe. How is it fair he is so pretty? I can't think straight when they are all here. "I will help with this training. I have a few ideas."

Why did that sound dirty? Why do I like the idea of training alone with them both?

I bite my bottom lip and I notice Lysander's eyes drop to my lips for only a second. "What's been happening since I left? Where have you been these last few months?"

"The sorcerer had the castle secured, and he kept us trapped in the castle while he attacked our people," Arden states. My eyes widen. They were trapped for months. Months.

"How did you get out?"

They all look at Arden. "I broke my cage, freed the others, and we managed to get out. We got lucky." He looks away from me, too quickly. He's lying and I can see it. I will bring that up with him when we are alone because it matters, what actually happened. "What about you?"

I tell them everything that has happened up to finding Hope and Livia. "Hope and Livia are alive." I watch Lysander, but he doesn't react at all to the news his girlfriend is alive. "I think the castle brought them here. I don't know why."

"I'm glad they're alive," Emrys tightly replies, also noticing how Lysander doesn't seem to care.

After a tense silence, I change the subject. "How did you get the tsar to agree to make an alliance with you? As far as I can tell, they hate magic, and dragon shifters are an insult to their own dragons."

Grayson grumbles. "I wanted to kill him, but Emrys insisted on making an alliance."

"I'd prefer him dead," Arden announces. "His brother too. I don't like how he looks at Elle."

They all seem to agree on that one, even Lysander. Emrys sighs. "Killing him would achieve nothing. The people would just pick another leader. There used to be cities here before the sorcerer attacked them. He destroyed hundreds of thousands of them before coming after our ancestors. They want him gone just as much as we do. Whether we'll still have arguments afterwards remains to be seen. We made an agreement that we will open our lands to them. That there will be no restrictions between us. We also made agreements that we would give them a considerable amount of money and help them build new cities. They're never quite rebuilt after the attack, and their people need a home."

Arden makes flames flicker over his fingers. "He has family to think of, and he agreed. We have you and our people to think of. They are being slaughtered by the sorcerer, and his army can help stop that. His dragon riders will be useful in what is to come."

Grayson rises, coming to me. He stands so close. Lysander walks out without another word. I bet he is going to see Hope. At least she will be happy, even if my insides turn to stone at the thought of him going to her. What is wrong with me? Grayson looks my way. "You should get some sleep, brat. Tomorrow is another day, and apparently, you're going to be a dragon rider."

Arden laughs. "Being a dragon rider has a whole different meaning in the courts. You can always be my dragon rider, princess."

Emrys makes a gust of wind knock Arden off his feet, and my lips twitch. I glance at the only bed in the room. "There's only one bed."

Arden is on his feet, a light growl at Emrys before he is in front of me. He picks me up and throws me over his shoulder. "It's a good thing we can share a bed, princess."

CHAPTER 8

"*I* need some fresh air." I stand in the middle of the room, refusing to go anywhere near the bed. "I can't go to sleep yet. I'm just—"

"Overwhelmed?" Emrys gently finishes my sentence when I can't. He looks worried about me, and I can't exactly tell him not to be. I'm worried, for more than one reason. From everything that happened in the courts to the fact I can't leave here without being a dragon rider. "You know we won't let you die in this rider challenge."

I don't say anything, but I rub my arm. "I almost died in the earth test. I was close to dying." I look at Arden. "Your ring saved my life." He looks at my hand where the ring is, but it doesn't glow anymore.

"I haven't had a chance to process any of that, let alone worry about what tomorrow is going to bring with the dragons. The commander said a lot of riders die, so how exactly is anyone going to keep me safe from those wild creatures?"

Arden takes a step closer, but I take a step away. I'm not sure how to deal with all of this, and I need some fresh air. "We are dragons, Ellelin. I know we have given you little reason to trust us, but we came here for you. We are focused on keeping you alive."

I don't want to ask why. I can't yet. I only nod and head to the entrance. Fresh air and a walk always clears the mind best.

I look back once, and Gray catches my eye. He has been so silent, and I just want to hug him. I want to comfort him, even when things are so fucked up between us. Falling for any of the dragon kings was never something I predicted would happen, but the moment I saw them today, I realised I have feelings for them. For each of them, except Lysander. I'm sure I hate him as much as I ever did. Gray raises one perfect eyebrow. "Don't go far. We can't trust everyone in this camp."

"I won't," I promise, knowing he needs me to say it. I painfully pull my eyes from him and head out, hearing them talking the second I'm out of the tent. Crossing my arms, I head to the left and through a few tents to a quiet part of the camp. There is nothing but darkness, the cavern walls at my side and the distant noise of the dragons and riders. Closing my eyes, I suck in a deep breath of the air. It's the perfect temperature down here, where I don't need to wear a coat as I continue to walk, my thoughts consumed with the kings and the fear of the dragons. The fear of the sorcerer who clearly wanted me dead. What happens when he catches up to us and goes for me again?

The dragons' roars echo across the distance, and I only get a few more feet before someone grabs me roughly, pinning me against the wall. "I can smell your fear miles away, darling."

My breath leaves my lungs as my back presses against the cavern wall, which is freezing to the touch. It takes me a minute to realise it's Lysander, and something about that fact doesn't scare me half as much as if it was someone else. He holds me against the wall with his own body. Everything about his firm, tall body is pressed against mine, so I'm forced to feel every hard inch of his body and how it fits so perfectly against mine. In the dim light, the shadows make his red hair shine like a light in the fire, and his eyes are so green like an endless sea that I feel trapped in when he looks right at me. "What do you want?"

He puts a single finger against my lips. My lips seem to come to life with that single touch, and my heart beats that much faster. Not in fear, to my shame, but I hope he thinks it's in fear. I hope he can't see everything that my body is screaming written across my face. "Quiet, we don't want anyone coming to rescue you from me."

"Fuck you," I snarl. "Let me go. What the hell do you want? Why are you bothering me? Did you see Hope, and did she piss you off or something?"

A smirk lines his handsome face. "Careful now. You sound jealous, Elle."

I scoff. "Jealous of you? That's insane. I'm not interested in you. Never. I'd never, ever go there with you." I push my face closer to his, fury spreading like water through my veins. "I hate you."

Lysander pushes into me, and his hardness presses into my stomach. Heat floods down my body in response as my eyes widen. "Liar. My enemy is a very, very bad liar." He brushes my hair over my shoulder, moving his face inches from my neck. I can't move, I can hardly think straight. "You looked relieved when you saw me today. Relieved I wasn't dead. Enemies don't look like you did."

"No." He is right. I'm a liar. I was relieved and I hate myself for it. This asshole blackmailed me into making Arden fall for me so I could kill him and break his heart. This asshole threatened to kill my grandmother. He is a monster, a villain, a disloyal bastard...and I was relieved he wasn't dead. What the fuck does that say about me? Denial is the best way forward, permanently.

He chuckles, moving back slightly but not letting me go. Steering the conversation away from my feelings, I ask, "Are you here to make sure our deal is still on? Because I think we are far past that." Lysander's expression changes. It's almost like he just remembered that we aren't friends. "Oh, have you decided not to kill one of your best friends? Someone who's like a brother to you? Someone who just got you out of a cage and saved your life?"

He growls at me, his grip punishing. I have the urge to growl right back at the bastard. His eyes look right down at me, and I hate that someone decided to give the villain the most beautiful eyes I've ever seen. The devil, that's what he is. I'm no longer willing to let myself care even an inch about his life. He somehow surprises me. "The deal isn't on anymore, because I've learnt it's not

Arden who I need to kill for what happened. It's you."

My lips part. I don't understand him. "Explain it to me. Explain why whatever happened is my fault?"

I don't get it. I have never understood why he would want Arden hurt and dead. If it was just about taking the Fire Court, maybe I could have understood it more, but it's not just that. This is personal for Lysander. "I always blamed Arden's father for killing mine, but it was your father who killed mine. I thought there was no one left to blame in the fifth court. No one I could kill to make up for what happened to my father, but here you are. My beautiful enemy." His eyes are so full of fury that a part of me is scared of him. "I already hated you from the moment we met, but I couldn't understand why I gave a shit about a little human that just walked into our life. Now I realise why." He growls low. "The obsession was there because the world was screaming at me that it was all your fault. Your father killed mine."

"I don't believe that," I counter. "Why is that what you believe? From what the others said, the Water Court king came to try to help my family to stop the sorcerer. Your father came to try to help

95

and ended up dead like mine. Like Arden's and Emrys's and Grayson's mother. No one is to blame other than the sorcerer! I was a fucking child!"

"So was I!" he roars, and I blink. He calms his voice slightly as he continues, "Arden's father decided that he was going to involve the Water Court with what was going on in the Spirit Court. He dragged him there. My father didn't want to leave. I was there. I remember all of it even when I wish I didn't. I begged my father not to go to that war. I knew he wouldn't come back. The waters had told me as much. The waters warned him too, but he said he couldn't leave them to fight alone. Arden's father told him he had no choice but to fight. It was a death sentence to go to the Spirit Court right then. The sea waters were screaming at him not to go. I was screaming at him not to go, and he still went."

My heart shatters. I can just imagine this little red-haired boy screaming for his father not to leave, not to die. "Lysander—"

"Don't you dare feel fucking sorry for me," he growls. "Get that look out of your eyes."

I can't. We both know I can't. I wonder if I begged for my mum and dad not to fight. It's only natural for a child to do that. "Arden's father pushed me back, and he wouldn't let me go with my father

96

to fight. He told Arden to hold me back. Arden did what he was told. He stood there, and he made me watch my father leave for the very last time."

"That's why you hate him, because he stopped you from going with your father," I whisper. "You blame him, but Arden was a kid too." I close my eyes. "I don't think anyone could have stopped your father, and I'm so sorry, Lysander. None of us will ever know what happened that day, twelve years ago, but they seemed to have stopped the sorcerer so you could grow up, so you could live. Can't you see it, that your dad sacrificed himself to save you? To save your mum, to save your brother and your court?" I reach out and touch his shoulder. "None of us is to blame, Lysander."

Lysander reaches out, wrapping his hand around my throat. "Shut up. You're wrong and you're not getting into my head. They're dead. He's dead. My mother never recovered. She was a shell for years afterwards, and my brother doesn't even remember our father. Should I not be angry? My mother is missing. My brother is missing. They're probably both dead. The Water Court is being raided. My people, who I'm sworn to protect, are being slaughtered for just being loyal to me. I'm not there, I'm here. All of it was for nothing because the sorcerer is out because of you."

Tears fill my eyes. "Lysander—"

"Are you telling me I shouldn't be angry?"

He loosens his grip. Not that he really hurt me to begin with. "I'm not telling you that you shouldn't be angry, but that isn't fair. You can't blame me for everything."

Lysander watches me so closely. "I think you're lying. I think you knew exactly who you were. It's why the castle helped you around. It's why I listened to you. You were born there, and the fifth court was always so mysterious. You can't know nothing."

"I did not know."

"Is that why you're hiding your power? To trick me?" His hand is still around my throat, but he never actually hurts me. He could kill me. We both know it, but he doesn't. That makes me hate him even more sometimes. He moves his face so close to mine. So, so close. Until we're just inches away from each other. I hate whatever this is between us. It pulls me back to him, time and time again, until I feel like I'm going mad because I have feelings for this fucked-up asshole. His lips are so close, and all I can breathe in is his sea salt, midnight scent. My mind and body betray me, working together to figure out what to do if he kissed me. To imagine what it would be like kissing him. It would be all fury and hate and anger, but I imagine he would kiss me better than anyone else.

"No," I snap. "I hate you. Let me go."

He growls at me again; this time I feel the growl echo through my body. He leans down even closer. So close that he is one breath away from kissing me, with his hand wrapped around my throat, his hard cock pressing into my stomach. I wouldn't stop him. We both know I wouldn't stop him kissing me. "The feeling is completely mutual, spirit witch. Whatever this spell you've put on me is, fucking stop it."

"I was right. You are fucking, you assholes!" Hope's shout makes me jump. Lysander instantly lets me go, turning to face Hope with me. "I knew there was something going on with you two."

"Hope," I whisper, seeing tears forming in her eyes.

She hastily wipes them away. "I knew it. I knew the second that I saw you two together that you wanted her. You denied it! You both denied it!"

Lysander looks bored. "I told you it was over before the earth test, Hope. I was honest with you from the beginning that it wasn't serious between us. Either way, nothing is happening between her and me."

Hope's eyes flash with anger and pain. Trust Lysander to make this so much worse. "I don't care. I'm done playing second choice. You stay the hell away from me, both of you."

She storms off into the main part of camp. I look at Lysander. "Are you going to go after her? She is upset."

He walks in the other direction with a yawn. "No."

"You're such a prick," I shout at his back, only making him laugh before I run after Hope.

I catch up with her just before she goes between two brown tents. She turns back to me. "What do you want?"

Her cheeks are covered in tears. I hold my hands up. "I'm sorry. That was…I don't know what it was, but it's not happened before. I never touched him before. I want you to know that."

She sarcastically laughs. "Sure, but you wanted him? I knew you did, and I knew he wanted you." I don't know what else to say. She goes to walk away and then turns back. "He is going to break your heart. Lysander told me once he believes that destined mates still exist in the world, and he wants his. He'll never be loyal to anybody but this imaginary mate that he believes exists."

Destined mates? I've never even heard of that. I want to ask her what that is, but she is still shouting at me. "He stopped wanting me not long after he started his fixation with you. I've wanted him since the first moment we met. I've loved him since, and I'll always love him. You might be his latest obsession, but that will soon pass. Whenever we get back to the courts, he will need a queen, and it won't be you. You won't choose him over the others, and he will hate you so much that he will want me again."

Crossing my arms, I watch her. "Hope, maybe he just isn't for you. I'm not saying I want him, but you deserve better."

She laughs with hate in her eyes. "You don't know anything about me. You're just a betraying, backstabbing bitch. I came to find you to warn you that the commander is dragging us all out early to the dragons. Apparently, the need for riders is higher than ever and they can't waste time. I came to help you. Fuck, I'm stupid. We aren't friends. You don't know how to even have a friend. No wonder Arty betrayed you."

Her words hit home because she is right. I've

never had friends, and everyone I've had so far has betrayed me. Hope walks away from me, and I bury my face in my hands. I just keep fucking up, and I'm sure when I face the dragons tomorrow, I'll do the same.

CHAPTER 9

There's one bed. One massive bed, but it would be hard to sleep in it with two dragon kings and not touch them. Accidentally or on purpose. I'm really, really not sure about sleeping in between them both and testing my self-control. I finish changing into one of Arden's shirts in the bathroom at the back of the tent, which is nothing more than a makeshift toilet and shower in the corner, and a bowl full of running water from a stream below so I can brush my teeth. I tug at Arden's shirt, which doesn't fall lower than my knees, but it only bounces back up to my upper thighs.

My heart is already racing when I leave the

bathroom and walk into the main area of the tent. Emrys is already in bed, lying on his stomach, reading a book in front of him. I climb into bed, glancing around for Arden and Gray, but I don't see them. Emrys is shirtless, but the blanket covers up most of his back. I can still see his rippling muscles and glimpses of a tattoo that seems to be on his ribs and curls around his side, but I can't see all of it. "What are you reading?"

He closes the book and hands it to me, leaving his page marked with a red bookmark. I read the title, *Histories of Greeks*. When I frown at him, he lies his head down. "On Earth and here, there is a lot of history on the Greeks and the gods they worshipped. I found this book here. There is a library mostly on combat and dragons, but this book stood out to me. What do you know about them?"

"Erm…" I pause, thinking back. My grand-mother loved the Greek gods, and she used to tell me such odd stories about them. Almost like she knew them. "My grandmother taught me about the main gods. Hades, Persephone, Demeter, Aphrodite, Ares, Poseidon, Zeus, Apollo, Athena, and Hera. Hera was my grandmother's favourite. She spoke about her a lot."

"Hera is the goddess of women and family."

Emrys smiles at me, and I hand the book back. That's not what my grandmother used to tell me about Hera. She spoke of her having incredible power over people. How she could persuade people to do what she wanted or forget anything she wished. Emrys reaches out, picking up my hand and linking our fingers. "Are you angry at her for not telling you the truth?"

"Livid," I softly admit. "I've looked up to her for my entire life, and the thought that she was lying to me… I can't process it. She has always been the most trustworthy person I've ever met. Now…I'm not sure what I can trust. Who I can trust."

"Me," he firmly suggests, touching my cheek. "But no one can tell you who to trust. That decision lies with you."

I lie down on the pillow in the middle of the bed, facing him. His green eyes are soft, gentle, like a breeze. Yet his scent reminds me of lilies and a storm in the middle of the day when all is meant to be quiet. His soft white-blond hair falls over his forehead as he looks at his book, leaning it on his impressive chest. My entire body twitches in excitement when I look at him, and I feel like whispering to my vagina, *Down, girl. Calm down.* "Emrys—"

Arden jumps into bed next to me, over six feet

of muscles and golden, damp skin. His hair is slightly wet, and he runs his hand through it as he looks over at us. "Is Emrys reading you a boring bedtime story on history?"

Reaching past me, he leans his hard chest across my back and plucks the book out of Emrys's hands, placing it on the side. "I actually like history," Emrys retorts.

Arden winks at me. "Sure, and I like when my dragon decides to eat sheep for dinner and makes me feel full so I can't eat anything half decent."

My eyes widen as he tucks himself under the blanket, his feet touching mine. I'm hyper aware of the little touches, the occasional brush of our hands or any part of our bodies. Trying to distract myself, I blurt out something random. "Did you fly here from the courts?"

Emrys answers, "Yes. My dragon was a bit confused when we met some wild dragons. They are smaller than us and they so far have stayed far away. I'm glad we got here to you. Lysander's sense of direction worked well."

"Lysander found me?"

Arden answers me this time. "Yes. I wanted to search further west, but he was absolutely adamant that we had to come this way. I assume he sensed the dragons and hoped you'd be with them."

"I'm still surprised he came with you at all," I admit.

"He was worried," Emrys tells me. "I know him, and he cares. He just doesn't know how to be a normal person about it."

I shake my head. He isn't a normal person and Emrys doesn't know him all that well. He doesn't know how he wants Arden dead, and now he wants me dead instead. Arden touches my arm. "Did you see Lysander on your walk?"

I hate lying to him, but explaining anything about Lysander would hurt him. He would be heartbroken to learn the truth of why I got close to him in the beginning and what Lysander was doing. "Nope. Where's Gray?"

"Are you going to tell us how you got him to hold your hand?" Arden outright questions. Emrys looks very interested too. I shake my head and he sighs. "Fine, keep your magic tricks to yourself. Gray said he didn't want to sleep, and he wanted to patrol the camp, get a good sense of what is in store for you tomorrow."

"Death, with my luck," I mutter.

Emrys picks up a strand of my hair. "Death doesn't get to claim you when you are ours, Ellelin. If it dares to try to take you, there will be four dragons burning the hand of death to ash."

My cheeks grow hot, a flush blazing throughout my body.

"You've made her blush, Em."

"Good, it suits her," Emrys responds, his eyes running down my body, to my bare legs. Even under the blanket, I feel like he can see all of me.

Arden places his massive hand on my stomach, spreading out his fingers, and heat flares from underneath his touch. I gulp. "I really, really like you in my clothes, princess."

"Wear mine tomorrow," Emrys possessively demands. Under both of their intense stares, I can't even breathe, let alone agree to anything. Emrys leans close to my shoulder, brushing my hair away from my neck. "You like us both, don't you? You want Gray too."

"I—yes," I mutter as he moves so much closer, his lips brushing against my neck. Not kissing me, not quite, but it's so much more teasing than I could imagine.

Arden softly pushes up my T-shirt, and my breath hitches. I pull my bottom lip between my teeth, and Arden watches, desire flaring in his eyes like bright flames. "Humans are so serious about only having one person to share their life with, but we prefer to do everything together. Including this. Including you. Our dragons can share, only between us, and we want you so badly."

Emrys kisses my neck, his lips soft but bruising with the pressure of each kiss. "I want to see you come around Arden's hand, mouth or cock with your lips on mine."

Arden runs his hands up my thighs, and I barely noticed him move to kneel at my side. "Say yes to us, princess."

I haven't had an orgasm in ages. An orgasm is exactly what I need to get some sleep, because I've been so fucking stressed, but then I've never been with two people at one time and…it seems like it would be more with them, more than just an orgasm. There's the two parts of me that are arguing with each other. Logic and my vagina. Of course, the urge for an orgasm wins. Because what girl would say no? I nod once at Arden, and Emrys hums against my neck, turning my head to the side to face him as Arden slowly pulls down my underwear. I gasp against Emrys's lips as Arden parts my legs, and I can feel him looking down at me. "Fuck, you're gorgeous. I need to taste you."

Emrys groans as I slide my hand down between our bodies, stroking him over his trousers. He is long, thick, and I grab him as Arden licks me once. Just once, parting me with his tongue before sucking on my clit. I moan loud, unable to hold back, and my other hand digs into Arden's hair as he devours my pussy like it's his last meal. Emrys turns my head back to him, kissing me deeply with his tongue, matching Arden. I can't think, only feel, and I'm so close. Arden pushes one finger inside me, and my pleasure rockets, but he doesn't let me go over the edge. Not yet. I moan around his finger, and he pulls it out, only to add another, making me feel fuller. I want more. I move my hips against his hand as he fucks me with his fingers, and Emrys devours my mouth. Emrys pushes my shirt up, revealing my breasts. He kisses down my jaw, rolling my hard nipple. "I think she needs your cock, Arden."

"Do you want my cock, princess?" Arden asks, still fucking me with his fingers. "Or do you want to come on my fingers first?"

God, I can't think. "I—"

Arden chuckles and I hear him pushing down

his boxers before grabbing my hips and lining us up. He looks down at me, rubbing the tip of his thick cock down my slit and back up. I'm so close, so, so close. He leans over me, but not before putting his thumb on my clit. As Arden slowly, torturously fills me, he rubs my clit until I'm blind with pleasure. I cry out as my orgasm pounds through me, and Arden fills me at the same time with his cock, until I'm full of him. So full. I'm shaking with pleasure as Arden holds onto my hips and slides out before ramming all the way back into me. "Shit, you're tight. You grip my cock so good, baby."

"You look *so good* when you're being fucked, Elle," Emrys groans against my neck as Arden pounds into me. It feels so, so good too. "I could come just watching him fuck you."

"God," I moan, the sensation of them both just so much. Emrys undoes his trousers and wraps my hand around his cock before kissing my sensitive nipple. I gasp and stroke his cock, wanting more. I don't want this to end.

Arden catches my gaze, his hands digging into my hips as he utterly destroys me with pleasure. "Come again, princess. I want to see how good you are at coming around my cock and making me fill you."

Somehow his words do just that. His thumb strokes my clit, Emrys's lips suck and tease my nipples, and I'm crashing into a mind-blowing second orgasm, tightening around Arden's cock and feeling him growing big, harder, inside me before he pauses. His cum is hot, and I feel impossibly full when he roars as he finishes in me, only extending my own orgasm. Emrys groans against my nipple, coming in my hand, and only then do I let myself breathe. That was unforgettable...and I want to do it again. Arden pulls out of me and Emrys makes two towels float over to us with his power. I go to catch one, but Arden gets it first and surprises me by cleaning me up before himself. Emrys pulls my shirt down and cuddles me, kissing my cheek. "You're amazing, Elle."

Arden climbs into bed, facing me. His hand rests on my side. "No regrets?"

I yawn, touching his cheek. "No. I want this, you, Emrys...all of this. Also, that was the best sex I've ever had."

Arden grins like he just won the lottery. Emrys whispers in my ear, "That sounds like a challenge."

I laugh and cuddle up with them both, feeling

impossibly safe. Arden and Emrys fall asleep pretty quickly, and I spend some time just enjoying being in their arms.

I'm starting to drift off with them both when Lysander walks in. His eyes find mine and he sniffs the air, anger burning in his eyes. I stay curled up on Arden's chest, Emrys's arm wrapped possessively around my waist. Lysander isn't going to make me feel bad. Lysander angrily pulls out the bed cushions to make some sort of makeshift bed and lies down on them without a blanket, his arms crossed.

"Witch, I turn you on and you use them for release. Very nice." His voice speaks directly into my mind, and I nearly gasp from the shock of it. I've heard him in my mind before, but never so direct. It was always when my life was in danger. I thought I was going mad, imagining him talking to me. But this is different. He's looking right at me with so much hatred in his eyes. He just spoke in my mind. How is that possible? I have to find out how he can do that and how to stop it.

I wonder if I can do it back. I think of Lysander and in my mind, I picture him as a sea of water, a violent and angry sea that is unpassable. Something snaps into place, and it feels as easy as breathing to speak right back to him in my head. "So judgmental for someone who doesn't want to join in. Jealous, my enemy?"

He blinks once, pure shock registering on his face. Maybe he didn't mean to say those things to me. Maybe he didn't mean to think them or say them into my mind. "Go to sleep, witch."

With my enemy watching me, I do just that.

CHAPTER 10

"Do you trust me?" Grayson demands, standing in front of a shard of light cutting through the rocks that makes his soft brown hair glimmer. His eyes are molten ash, watching me calmly. He hasn't spoken to me much this morning. I'm not sure when he got back, but he was sleeping on the spare floor cushions when I woke up. We had a quick breakfast, which was a mixture of breads and cheese. It wasn't great food, but I wasn't expecting much, travelling out in the desert. After cleaning up, we left the tent. Arden went off with Lysander, and Emrys and Grayson led me away. Gray found this ledge away from the camp, and it is pretty deserted. He patiently waits for my answer as I watch him. I can tell he hasn't slept much, but I think suggesting perhaps he go have a nap will not go down well. He looks pissed and I get it. We really do need to talk alone, but Emrys is standing at his side, looking between us with a mix of curiosity and some humour. My cheeks just burn when I think of last night.

"Of course I do. I trust you, Gray." I relax my shoulders and sit down, like he asked me to do earlier. Dark ivy vines shoot out of the sandy ground, stretching up and wrapping quickly around my arms and legs, holding me in place. From the vines, small exotic flowers slowly burst out of them, slowly growing into huge flowers. "Whatever you're doing is beautiful."

Grayson's lips twitch but his eyes are closed while he is concentrating. Grayson barely moves as he's using his power to create massive trees in a circle around us both, the leaves of the trees blocking us from any view. His power is inspiring and yet he barely moves while he does it. Will I ever have power and control over magic like this? The flowers are beautiful exotic-looking yellow and orange flowers that slowly wrap around my wrists and arms, smothering my skin. Grayson keeps his eyes shut, but he is stretching his hand. Emrys takes the cue. He clicks his fingers. Wind whips around my skin, wrapping around every inch of me to feel the cold current of it blowing across my body.

I want to ask what they're doing, but I can see they're both concentrating. I let myself relax, knowing deep in my soul that neither of them would hurt me. They came for me. They are staying for me. Suddenly, the magic stops. The vines fall away, the wind disappears, and the petals of the flowers fall into my lap before turning into sand that blows away from my hand. Emrys and Gray look at each other for a long time, another silent conversation that speaks volumes. Gray turns to me and runs a hand through his hair, which is shorter since the tests. Lysander wasn't the only one who cut their hair recently. "There's strange magic wrapped tightly around you."

"What do you mean? Where did it come from, and can you get rid of it?"

Emrys offers me his hand, and I take it, standing up. The petals blow away in the wind. "I can sense the magic, and it is connected to your very soul. It's faint, different from anything I ever felt before, and it protects you. I've studied all the courts' magic, except the Spirit Court, but this was not a magic born of darkness and shadow. To remove it…"

"It might kill you. It's linked to you, whatever

this magic is," Grayson finishes. Wow. Okay, so we aren't doing that.

I rub my forehead. "What if my parents put this magic on me and they are the only ones who can take it away? Does it mean I'm stuck like this forever? Weak and useless with no magic even when my parents were—"

"You are not useless or weak," Emrys stops me, stepping closer and cupping my cheeks. "You are one of the strongest people I've ever met. Don't you dare think for a second that magic would change anything about you. Power is inherited in our world, and it means you will have magic, but for some reason you cannot access it."

I pull away from him. I know he means well, but my court is dead, my parents are dead, and the person who slaughtered them is going to come after me. I can never avenge them; I can't even protect myself. I was used to being human, but I never felt like I fit in; I felt odd. Now that I know the truth, I can't go back. I want my magic. I need it. "It would change everything for me. Ever since you kidnapped me, I've felt weak and tiny in this world, but now...I know that I wasn't born to be that. I want to avenge my parents and stop the sorcerer. I want to be able to protect myself and make my

COURT OF DRAGONS AND VOWS

parents proud. They died for me! They put all their hope in me, and if I do nothing but hide behind you four, then I've let them down. I've let myself down."

Gray looks right into my eyes. "We will kill him together, and this was just the beginning. I will find a way and you will be at my side."

"We can call it a bonding moment to make him suffer. He killed our parents too," Emrys says with a gentle smile, trying to calm me with some humour. It almost works.

My shoulders drop. I know it wasn't just my parents. "I'm sorry. I just hoped it would be easy and I could begin learning to use my powers."

Emrys strokes my arm. "I know, Elle. The tsar imported a lot of books, books I've never seen in the courts, and I read a lot. I'm going to go and continue reading. Maybe I can find something about this magic hold on you. I think I'm missing something." He looks at Gray. "Look after our girl."

"Always," he answers, but he is tense, more when Emrys kisses my cheek. Emrys leaves through the forest of new trees around us, and soon I hear a familiar dragon roar and then see a flash of scales through the thick trees. Gray and I look at each other. I'm not sure whether I should speak first or I should let him. He is wearing black clothes under a cloak, no armour because he doesn't need it. "Do you love Arden?"

I'm a little shocked by the question. "I don't think telling you my feelings before I admit it to him is fair." I step forward. "Gray, I remember what you said. You want me as yours, not theirs…but I can't do that. I care about you all, and I don't want to hurt anyone. Perhaps I should ask for another tent and—"

"No," he cuts me off, taking another step closer until his scent wraps around me. Sandalwood and forests, both scents that I enjoy but even more from him. Grayson reminds me of the forest, a thick forest you could stroll into and get lost without realising it. "I love you." My breath hitches and my heart pounds. This is the first time someone has told me they love me, and it's something I wanted. My ex told me it over and over, but it was just words. I didn't know it could feel like this. There is so much conviction in those three words from him. He means each word with every bit of his soul. "When I was young, I was taught love was cruel and punishing. I was made to believe that loving anyone was a punishment, because they do nothing but cause you pain. I have never felt remotely interested in anybody until you made me see that love is more than that. Now you're all that I can think about, all that I dream about, and you deserve so much better than me. You deserve someone like Arden or Emrys. They're perfect for you, and because of that, I'm going to stay away—"

I close the gap between us and kiss him. Grayson's entire body tenses against me for a second. Have I pushed him too far? I can't make myself regret it. Then he snaps. Grayson groans against my lips, kissing me back with such furious passion that I can hardly breathe, hardly think of anything but him as he grabs my shirt and pulls my body against his. He picks me up, cupping my ass and pressing my back against the tree. His lips trail down my jaw, down my neck, pulling at my shirt. He suddenly stops, dropping me and backing away. We stare at each other as I try to get my breath back. That has to be the best kiss I've ever had. Ever.

"I fell for you when you talked me through my panic attack," I confess. "I never told you the truth, that I was beaten nearly to death and Lysander healed me. He then killed the person who hurt me, Desmerda. I was so scared, and you pushed through everything you fear to comfort me. I think that was the moment I knew I loved you, and it broke me, broke me, to not be able to just kiss you like that."

"Kiss me, touch me, I'm yours," he breathlessly vows. "I'm not perfect. I'm scarred but yours. Broken but yours." He pushes up his shirt and shows me the many, many cuts littering his arms. I gasp, covering my mouth as tears fill my eyes. It looks like someone cut him over and over again. "You shouldn't want me."

"Gray. You don't get to tell me who or what I want, and you certainly don't get to put yourself down in front of me. I can see you, you know, past everything, past all the defences, everything you put there in order to protect yourself from the world. I see all of it, and I still love you," I admit. "When I see your scars, I want to kiss each one and erase every negative thought you have about them. One day, I want to know what happened to you, but not today. Today is our first kiss, our first moment that's real."

Grayson's eyes are speaking a million things, but he simply nods once and changes the subject. "While Emrys reads, we will continue our training."

I smile. "I'd like that."

Before Grayson says anything else, the commander steps through the trees. He looks between us, his eyes tense. "There you are, King Grayson." Sarcasm laces his words before he informs me, "My brother has insisted we take the dragon trials forward. The dragons are unusually restless. The quicker that you bond with your dragon, the quicker we can make formations, train you, and go back to the courts to take them over again."

Grayson looks down at me. "Are you ready for this?"

"Is anyone?" I question. "But yes."

We follow the commander out of the trees, and the branches hit him more than once but never touch us. I shake my head at Grayson, and he winks at me once. When the commander is out of the new forest, he grumbles, "Fucking trees."

"They can hear you," Grayson warns, his voice cold. He looks down at me, his tone much softer. "We'll meet you there. I'll find the others."

The commander waves towards the camp, and Grayson stays at my side until we are at the crowds in the middle area. He leaves as I join the back of the group, spotting Livia and Hope nearby. Hope looks at me with such hostility that Livia notices and looks between us. She comes over to stand by my side. "You alright? Where did you sleep?"

Hope doesn't follow her over, and when I don't answer right away, she sighs. "I'm guessing whatever happened is the reason Hope came back in tears and cried all night."

I immediately feel bad, but I don't know how to fix it. "It was my fault. The dragon kings are here and I'm staying with them."

"Lysander," Livia sighs, crossing her arms. "This is why I prefer to date girls."

The commander claps his hands loud enough for all the chatter of the group to stop. There are two women standing behind him and Healer Ainela, who finds my eyes for a moment, but I'm soon distracted by the commander's explanation. "Here are your riding clothes, full leather that is fire and ice proof. Put these on, but remember that they may protect only some parts of your body. If a dragon burns or freezes you, the uniform will be all that's left. Also, it'll be cold when you're riding on the back of the dragon, but cloaks are not advised, as they can pull you off. Leave your cloaks in the tents." The commander points to his other side. "Here are your daggers. Your dragon will mark you, if you're not marked already, and you must mark the dragon right back. Three straight lines, like claw marks, on the side of their neck, in between the scales. This will bond you both and make you able to speak to them."

A man near the front shouts, "How do you know which dragon is yours?"

The commander looks right down at him. "You'll die if they're not yours. Fate always leads you to your dragon, but some of you won't survive either way. We will take you to the entrance, a place where the dragons want the riders to go. There's not much we can tell you or warn you of, but healers will be ready for those who fly."

"Good fortune to you all," Healer Ainela states before walking away with the commander, leaving the women to hand out daggers and clothes.

Livia leans into me as we join the makeshift line. "Do you think people died in those clothes, and they just plucked them up, washed them, and gave them to us?"

I grimace. "I'm just hoping they washed them."

Everyone around me looks as terrified as I feel, except a few that seem excited. They are morons. Something makes me look back to find Grayson, Emrys, Arden, and Lysander watching me. The full force of their gazes makes me shiver and turn back. Livia looks back once. "I'm guessing they are coming with us for you. I'm just glad I don't have to marry one of them now. It would have been a shock when I told them I like girls."

"I don't think anyone will be able to stop them," I reply as we get close to the front.

Livia leans into me. "Girl, how are you walking straight when all four of them are yours?"

I choke on thin air before laughing slightly. "We aren't...well, not yet."

Livia starts elbowing me in the ribs. "I want details. All the details."

Hope pushes my shoulder as she barges past me, looking back at me once before snatching a pile of clothes and a dagger from the woman. I don't bother arguing with her when she is like this and holding a dagger. I know there is nothing I can say. Instead, I pick up my pile of clothes and dagger after Livia and go with her into the female-only tents where the girls are getting changed. Everyone is getting changed in front of each other, and I feel a bit self-conscious as I start taking my clothes off. Pulling the tight leather on is more difficult than I thought it would be, but when I'm finally dressed, I buckle my belt and clip the dagger into a holder at the side so it falls next to my upper thigh. The leather is ridiculously tight, and it shows everything. Livia comes over, offering me a hair band. "Let me sort your hair out."

I smile warmly, turning, and she braids my hair for me. "I love how the black fades into purple. It suits you."

Glancing at the mirror on the wall, I pull the fishtail braid over my shoulder. The leather clothes make every curve of mine stand out, but the dark brown complements my skin tone, and the braid really does look pretty. "Thanks, Liv."

Hope walks past me towards the door and slams her shoulder into mine. "Watch it, bitch."

"Hope—"

She turns on me. "Don't you dare try to apologise or say anything to excuse yourself! I don't want to hear it!"

"ENOUGH!" Livia all but screams. Hope and I turn to face her. "That's enough from the pair of you. I had to lose the person I love in the earth test. I could not save her. She was dead. I had to run for my own life, and so many of us died. You forget that. We are lucky to be alive when they are not, and this is how you want to act? Like school kids arguing over a man? There's only three of us left, and we owe it to those who didn't make it not to be at each other's throats. We could die, once again, and you both need to grow up. We have bigger problems!"

Hope looks at me, and I blow out a breath. Hope snarls. "Fine, but we aren't friends. Not when she goes after other people's men."

"I didn't—"

"Enough!" Livia snaps once again. "Let's go and find out if a dragon wants us dead or alive."

Livia hooks her arm through both Hope's and mine, making it clear we aren't going anywhere separately. I get why Hope hates me, and Livia is right about most of it, except that there aren't three of us left from the Crown Race. There are four, but Arty isn't here fighting for her life. She is out there with her evil father.

Exiting the tents, we follow the crowd to the very front of the camp. Then we go down stone steps to a clearing under the campsite where there is a massive cavern entrance with smooth stone around the edges of the cavern. On the smooth stone are carved symbols, runes perhaps, but nothing I've seen before. The mark on my chest feels like it's alive, burning my skin, and I cover it with my hand over my leather clothes.

The commander whistles from the top of the steps that lead to the cavern entrance, and he holds his hand up as the group gathers around the bottom of the steps. Sickness rises in my throat because I've been in tests before and seen people die. I don't want to see it again; I don't want more nightmares that will forever haunt me, but once again, I don't have a choice.

"Go!" the commander demands. "Dragons wait for no mortals."

The crowd begins walking into the cavern until there are only a few left at the back with Hope, Livia, and me.

"Good luck, Hope," someone calls. I turn to see Arden smiling at her. She nods, looking once at Lysander, who doesn't so much as flinch. After Livia and Hope leave for the cavern, Gray speaks first. "We are coming with you."

The commander steps to my side, his arm brushing mine. I step aside. "You're not."

Lysander sounds bored. "I'll step over your dead body if you don't move."

The commander clears his throat. "This isn't my choice. The dragons are extremely possessive of their homes, and they will not accept you. There will be fights, and Ellelin is mortal. She will be caught up in all this fighting between dragons, and she will end up dead. We have a responsibility to respect the dragons' home that we are guests in. They have invited Ellelin here, not you."

Arden looks him up and down, and suddenly the surrounding air grows hot. Flames bounce around the ground under the commander's feet. "Move."

"No." They all turn to me. I step forward in front of the commander. Killing him would only piss off his brother, and he has a point. "I feel something in there, like the dragon is pulling me in. This is my battle. I know you want to protect me. I do get that, but you'd cause more danger for me by coming in there."

"I'd rather burn them all down than risk you," Arden responds.

I shake my head. "But I don't want that. One of these dragons saved my life and marked me. I won't return that debt by letting you slaughter them."

Arden's shoulders drop. "Fine, but you shout for us if you're in danger."

"I will."

"Be careful, brat," Gray warns. Emrys's eyes steadily meet mine, but he doesn't offer anything. We both know there isn't much to say.

As I walk past the commander, Lysander's voice fills my mind. "If you die, I'll hate you more."

My lips twitch and I'm thankful for the distraction. My legs are like jelly as I head into the cave, and I try to think of anything useful, but all that comes to mind is *Game of Thrones*, and a lot of people died in that from dragons. The dragons were cool, though. "Like I would ever want to displease you."

As I walk into the cavern, the first thing I see is a massive silver dragon swoop down in front of me and eat a woman with one flash of shiny teeth. She didn't even have time to scream.

CHAPTER 11

*F*ear forces me to be silent as I freeze, staring at the spots of blood on the ground where the woman just was. I can't move, I can't force my body to do anything. I need to make a plan and decide what I'm going to do next. One thing I've realised in all the tests, all the death that surrounds me, is that I don't want to die yet. I won't die yet.

A gold dragon swoops low, fire crackling out of its massive mouth before it drops its jaw, blue fiery flames shooting right towards me. I scream, jumping to the side, the flames licking my back, but my clothes protect me. I run. My legs move before my mind can catch up, and I barely have time to see the corner of the cavern wall before I almost crash into it.

Turning, I'm glad to see the dragon has left me alone and flown after the groups of people running from them on the other side of the cavern. More dragons, all silver and gold, leap out of hidden niches in the walls, surprising people and melting them to ash before they even notice the dragon above. They move so fast despite how big they are. Searching the bottom floor, I don't find Livia or Hope anywhere, but there are so many people running in so many directions.

This cavern has an entrance above, leading to the desert, and I spot a few new riders on the back of their dragons flying out. I need to find mine. Flames lick the ground, not just white flames but ice-cold ones too that leave frost in their wake. I stay close to the cavern wall, touching the rough rock with my hands as I go around the edges. I don't think running around out there is a good idea. Everyone must look like panicking bugs to the dragons. I follow the cavern wall around until I find a small, thin gap in the rock, big enough for me to slide through it. Something in my chest, in my mind, tells me to go through it.

Above the gap are gold symbols etched into the

G. BAILEY

wall, more of those runes. I slide through the gap, the rock walls painfully pressing into my skin and cutting my arms as I push through it. On the other side is a giant room with a puddle of green water in the middle. Water drops from somewhere high above, but I can't hear the sound over the echo of the dragon roars and human screams. I don't see any other exits, but I'm not going back through the gap. Rubbing my face with my sore hands, I look around and notice one of the walls has another gap, this one higher up. Ignoring the pain in my hands, I begin climbing up the wall, blocking out the sounds I'm still hearing. I think it will be worse when there is silence, because then, most of the people are dead.

"Come on, I can do this." Talking to myself seems to make my legs move. I don't know why I wasn't half as frightened in the Crown Race tests as I am now. Maybe the thought of a dragon eating me is more terrifying than anything I previously imagined. The rocks cut further into my hands until they are layered with blood, but I don't stop climbing until I can reach the ledge. After pulling myself up, I place my hands on my knees and take a deep breath, pushing away any self-doubt. I crawl through the smaller cavern tunnel to the other side,

134

where I can see darkness and, strangely, all I want to do is get to it. I step out onto hot sand that stretches in so many directions, and I can't see the edges of the cavern, as it is nothing but dark shadows.

Silver light pours down from above, and I look up. A glittering black sky stretches above me, but it's not sky at all, it's just black stone with crystals that look like stars sparkling within the rock. Light pours through the crystals, making the silver glow and pushing away the unnatural darkness that surrounds this place. A part of the ceiling is missing crystals, but then it moves. My heart pounds like a drum as the blackness moves.

Large, scaled wings stretch out, smothering the light as a pair of green, black-tipped eyes appear in the darkness. The dragon's eyes look like green stars in a dark sky, but then it roars, shaking the very walls, and darkness explodes around it, spreading across the walls and ceiling until everything goes dark. I straighten my shoulders in the darkness and close my eyes. I won't be afraid as I die. I hear the thump of the dragon as it lands near me, and I nearly fall over from the force. I hear it move closer, the heat of the dragon so different from the chill in the air. I don't open my eyes and I hold my head high as I feel and hear it sniff me.

When it hasn't moved for a while, I dare to open my eyes. There is a little light in the room now, enough for me to see the massive dragon right in front of me, holding my gaze. It's huge and I'd guess male. The dragon has a long tail that curls around its legs, filled with thorns like Arden's. Its mouth is full of sharp teeth that are silver, a contrast to his black scales. I slip out the dagger and hold it tightly in my hand. The dragon doesn't move. "You're the dragon who saved me, aren't you?"

Of course, the dragon doesn't answer, it simply watches me. Nervously, I place my hand on one of its scales, which is bigger than my hand. The second I touch it, the new marks on my chest almost seem to burn to life. The scales are sharp, every single one of them sharp at the end but softer at the top. "It only seems fair, you marked me. Apparently, this is what I have to do. I don't know shit about riding dragons, and my life is trouble. I'd understand if you didn't want me as your rider. You can leave if you want."

He doesn't move. This magnificent dragon stays for me. The dagger is shaking in my hand as I press it into the scales, into the space in between. His skin glitters, and it is hard, like leather. I won't draw blood with the cuts. I draw the first cut, and when I make the second, I feel something sharp cut deep through my chest, making me gasp. The pain is intense, like I can feel the cuts I'm making. That's impossible. My hand shakes as I make the third, last cut, and the second I lift the dagger away, the mark on my chest burns. I cry out, falling back straight into the sand as I clutch my chest. The terrible pain fades eventually, leaving me gasping on the sand, blinking at the strange feeling coursing through my body. I'm bonded to a dragon.

A deep male voice fills my mind. "You are my rider from now until I take my last flight from this world and beyond. I choose you, princess of the Spirit Court, because we were born to be one. Rise, we have a world to save."

My eyes widen as I climb to my feet, brushing off sand. "How did you know who I am, and what is your name?"

He rises up, towering over me. "Terrinyss. You can call me Terrin for short. We've waited a very long time for you to come for us and claim your people as your father once foretold."

My mouth is dry. "What?"

Terrin huffs. "Twelve years ago, your father transformed us all into dragons, bonded our souls to this form, and sent us over the seas to the west to save our lives. All seven thousand of us are here. The children have grown, like me. We were the same age when the court fell."

I'm too shocked to say anything, and I'm sure my mouth is hanging open as I stare at him. He can't be serious. "You're really from the Spirit Court? How would my father know I'd turn up here one day?"

"The prophecy told—"

"What prophecy?" I demand.

Terrin lies down, meeting my eyes again. "I was always meant to be yours; this was foretold. You came here. How do you not know this?"

I shake my head. "I didn't know I was from the Spirit Court, or that this world existed at all, until recently. I was brought up on Earth."

Terrin growls. "Then you have much to learn, my rider. Climb on. We must ride to deepen our bond."

He lowers his wing for me and patiently waits. I look at him once. "You're from my court?"

A hum from him fills my mind, and I nod, climbing up his side and onto his back, right between his scales. I clench my thighs as he stretches his wings out into the darkness, and he leaps into the air in one swoop. My stomach turns as I grip onto his thorns, the air whipping against my skin. Terrin crashes through the ceiling and right out into the hot desert, where the other dragons are flying with their riders. Terrin roars loudly, and they are all behind us as we fly through the sky. "I am from your court, Ellelin, and together we will bring war to the male who tried to destroy us."

CHAPTER 12

*W*e land with a thump in a massive clearing at the bottom of the cavern, where all the other dragons are landing. My hands are ice cold from the flight, even when we stayed above ground in the desert. I look up, far up, to where the camps are. I spot my dragon kings on the edge, looking right down at me. Together, they look invincible and, not for the first time, I wonder what they see in me. My heart leaps into my chest when Arden steps off the cliff edge, falling elegantly before shifting into his fierce black, red-tipped dragon. One by one, all the dragon kings jump into their massive dragons that spread their wings out and soar around the cavern together, collecting dragons to follow them.

Terrin's voice fills my mind. "They are kings to all dragons."

In this moment, I see it. The dragons around me roar as they look up, some almost seem like they hiss, but one by one, they incline their heads. All but my dragon, who watches them like they're his enemies. I pat his neck. "They're my friends."

"Liar. My senses are brilliant in dragon form." My cheeks burn at whatever he is scenting. "They are the others from the prophecy."

"What is this prophecy, Terrin?" I demand.

Terrin huffs, stretching out his wings. "You're not ready to hear the truth, my rider." I lean back, crossing my arms. I go to protest, but his voice fills my mind. "We all are together from now until time ends. We'll have plenty of moments for me to explain everything to you. First, you must learn to ride on my back so we can fight as a team. You nearly fell off. More than once. That will not do going forward with my plan."

"You're very cryptic, you know that?"

"It's almost as if my entire life was planned for this moment." He laughs in my head as he lowers himself down. "Your friends are over there with their weaker dragons."

"That's not very nice, Terrin." I follow the

direction of his head to see Hope on the back of a gold dragon that is long and has a massive tail compared to its thin body. I bet her dragon is fast. Behind her is Livia on the back of a silver dragon that is chunky, with smaller wings and a thin mouth. The silver one tips her side, forcing Livia to fall off the side of its wing and onto the ground. I don't need to be close to see the curses Livia is shouting with a mouth full of sand.

"It is true. The silver one is unpleasant and will not be trained easily. The gold has a temper," Terrin explains. "Troublesome dragons for your friends."

"They can handle themselves," I answer. I'm arguing with a dragon. I bet the dragon queen from *Game of Thrones* didn't have this issue. "So be nice. Please."

Terrin huffs a laugh before doing exactly what the silver dragon did to Livia. Terrin moves so quickly, lowering his wings and tilting his body so I have no choice but to roll off straight into the sand. I glare at my dragon as I stand up. "And you say *they* are troublesome? Are you kidding me?" I blow out sand from my mouth. "That wasn't funny!"

"It definitely was, my rider." Terrin spreads his wings out. "Watch your back in this camp. Burning it down in shadowflame wouldn't make anyone happy, but I will if anyone hurts you."

"What is shadowflame?" I shout, but he takes off, the force of air from his departure nearly knocking me over. Terrin flies high into the sky, straight after the dragon kings in the distance. Several of the dragons fly behind mine.

"So, you survived," Hope shouts over, gracefully sliding off the side of her dragon, touching it softly as I walk over. The dragon's gold eyes find mine, and a sharp pain touches the back of my neck. Rubbing the back of my neck, I stop, noticing Hope is doing the same. "What in the dragon was that?"

The dragon looks right at me. "This is your blood bound, Rider of Terrin. I am Dalinda."

Hope and I both look at the dragon. "What are you talking about? Are you talking to her?"

Dalinda sighs. "Two mortals who share blood. You are bound together and, therefore, I can speak to her. You will be able to speak to her dragon."

"I am not bound to her," Hope snarls. "The back of my neck is burning. Will you look?"

She turns and I see a Celtic circle with a dragon in the middle marked on her skin. I turn and Hope confirms what I suspect. "It's a circle with a dragon in the middle. Do I have the same?"

Turning back, I nod once. "Blood bound, how is that possible? What is that?"

Dalinda answers, although she sounds bored and annoyed. "It means you share blood. Not from being related, but from a choice made recently."

I think back, and it hits me. The air test. I grabbed her hand and both of us were cut from climbing the rocks. Our blood must have mixed then, but it was an accident.

"How the fuck do we undo that?" Hope shouts, crossing her arms and glaring at me. "Of all the fucking people, I had to take your bloody hand and bind us."

"I'm not interested in this either. How do we undo this, Dal?"

Dalinda huffs. "There is no undoing the work of the mighty dragon gods. Not everyone is bound with blood sharing. You have been picked and honoured." Dalinda nearly knocks over Hope as she spreads out her wings and flies off into the sky.

Awkwardly, Hope and I say nothing for a long time. I blow out a breath and face her. "I get that you hate me, but we clearly need to find a solution."

"Okay, don't date Lysander. Don't fuck him," she suggests, raising an eyebrow, but there is vulnerability in her eyes. Part of me wants to agree to her offer, but I won't. Hope needs to move on from Lysander; otherwise, anytime he so much as looks at someone else, this is going to happen again. She hasn't ever given me a reason to trust her, let alone agree to what she wants, but walking away from her doesn't seem like an option anymore, and I doubt I'll get Lysander out of my life anytime soon. Hope is right about one thing. Why the hell did we have to be bound together? If some dragon gods are doing this, what are they thinking?

"Hope, I—"

"Well done, our new riders!" Commander Ivan shouts from behind us. Hope looks away from me, tucking her braid over her shoulder. I turn, seeing Commander Ivan walking our way. He stops close to me. "A hundred and twenty-four riders have survived so far, but sometimes we have late riders come out. A brilliant turnout."

That means hundreds are dead. I don't know how many went in there, but I'd guess near to four hundred. Sickness rolls in my stomach as I remember the deaths I did see, the screams I did hear, and the fact he looks so damn happy about it. The Dragon Crown Race tests were different. The dragon kings didn't have a choice other than to make the test and sit at the sides. Thousands, millions, could die if they didn't. The commander and tsar have literally been kidnapping people from the courts and forcing them to do this for no other reason than war. *Brilliant* doesn't seem like the right word. He looks so happy that it makes my stomach churn. I look around for the riders I can see, looking for Cordelia. She had to have made it. "Ellelin, good I caught you. Can I speak to you alone?"

Hope steps to my side. "She doesn't want to speak to you alone." I'm surprised and silent as I glance at her. She's right though, I don't want to be alone with him. Something about him just creeps me out, and the fact he chose now, when the kings are distracted, bothers me more.

Commander Ivan looks down at her. "You're in my army, Hope. I never asked you. This is a private matter and above you."

"She tells me everything, so you might as well speak here," Hope deflects with a lie.

A lie the commander sees right through. "Just because you have a dragon now, it doesn't mean your life is safe. Do as you are told! Go and celebrate with the rest of your people before I decide to lock you up in your disobedience."

Hope looks at me, and I nod. She frowns and

looks at Commander Ivan. "They're not my people, but fine."

Commander Ivan waves towards the stone steps where he came from, and I walk with him, away from Hope, who is walking towards Livia. I glance up, looking for my own dragon, but I can't see much in the darkness here. It feels like we climb nearly three thousand steps straight up until we get to the camps, and my legs are like jelly, whereas Commander Ivan is fine. I need more cardio. The commander leads me to the tsar's tent. I'm relieved we won't be alone. It makes more sense why Hope couldn't come. She doesn't know the tsar. "Is your brother here?"

"No, he's returned to see his child and wife." He waves at one of the seats. Once again, I don't sit but stand next to it. I'm tempted to speak to Lysander and ask him to come here. Almost tempted, but the commander hasn't actually done anything to me other than make me feel uncomfortable. Some men just make me feel that way. I push my worries to the back of my head. He clearly wanted me here for a reason. "Family is important to us. It always has been. Before my brother met his wife, there were only us two after our sister was stolen and our parents killed by someone from the courts."

I don't know what to say. "I'm sorry that happened to you both."

Commander Ivan nods, watching me. "No one ever found our sister, and I believe my brother has hopes she is still alive in the courts somewhere. I don't think so." He clears his throat. "Now you know some of my truth. Perhaps we can talk more. You have considerable power over the dragon kings. I don't understand what you are to them, or how they are okay sharing you, but—"

I straighten. "I thought you had something important that you wanted to talk to me about. My relationship is not up for discussion."

He smirks and lowers his voice like I'm a child. "Oh, but Ellelin, this is important. Your relationship is important because you clearly have all of them wrapped around your finger. Or around your pussy." I wince at how brash he is and what he is accusing me of. "I can see that you like powerful men."

He starts to walk towards me, and everything in me tells me I should run. The commander reaches out, gripping my shoulder, and his grip is tight. "I would like to have a discussion with you about where you want to be when this is all over. Powerful men are in short supply, and I know that you have been forcibly taken into some sort of test that they did. But you don't belong to them. You don't have to be with them when—"

"Ellelin!" Emrys shouts from outside, right before he steps in. Relief floods my body. "There's my girl." He looks at my shoulder, the hand on my shoulder more like it, and his eyes flash white. The entire room goes colder as an icy wind whips around the tent. The commander lowers his hand immediately with a big, overly friendly smile. Emrys comes to my side, wrapping a possessive arm around my waist. Emrys always came across as a flirty, golden-retriever-type guy, but not right now. Now he is possessive and I'm glad for it as I lean back into him. "Thank you for your concern. I'm happy where I am."

Emrys kisses the side of my head. Commander Ivan clears his throat. "Well, I'm glad to hear it. Congratulations on your new dragon. We will fly together in training."

"You looked amazing on your dragon, sweetheart," Emrys offers. "He's nearly as big as mine."

"He's one of the biggest dragons left," the commander informs. "Terrin is the brother of my own dragon."

I look up at Emrys. "We should leave the

commander. I'm sure he has more important things to do."

Emrys doesn't bother saying goodbye and neither do I as he leads me out. I feel the commander's eyes on my back until we are outside. "Don't be alone with him again. He can't be trusted with you."

"I won't," I promise. I didn't get good vibes from him either. I remember everything that Terrin told me about the shadow dragons and how they're real people. I wonder if Commander Ivan knows that his dragon is actually a person trapped here by my own father. I doubt it. I'm sure that discussion would have come up if he knew that. "Why don't you show me this library you keep hiding in? I like books and I used to read sometimes. Although my books were more spice than story."

Emrys winks at me. "Tell me more about this spice? In detail...for my research."

I whack his chest, and he laughs, capturing my hand and kissing it. "Actually, I want to tell you about something else that happened when I was bound with my dragon. He's from my court."

Emrys links our fingers. "Explain that to me?"

"Terrin, my dragon, can talk to me." I almost

say *like Lysander does*, but I don't. "And he claimed he was from my court. Along with others."

"Mind talking is an unusual quality. I will have to have a look at it. I'm sure I was reading the book recently about mind talking, but it's slipping my mind what it was about." He rubs his face. "But tell me everything."

I tell him everything that I was told, prophecy included, and how Terrin said Emrys was part of it. "I wonder why he thinks you're not ready to hear it."

"Have you read or heard anything about prophecies?" I question.

"No, not exactly. I've heard of a prophecy, spread down from the mighty dragon gods to the people of the Twilight, the religious people in the courts, but I've never been the religious sort. I believe they only tell those who bind themselves to the Twilight what the prophecy is." Emrys frowns. "Arden might know more. His people are one of the more religious courts. But I don't know what the prophecy would be and why your father would bind them into dragons."

We head into a tent that immediately smells like old books and thick dust that you only get at libraries. This tent has been transformed into one.

Rows of old, nearly broken bookcases stretch down the middle of the tent, and they are filled with old books on their shelves. There are a few little tables spotted around between them, and it's empty in here besides us.

We go to the back, where a table is piled high with books, a few empty cups, and more cushioned seats around it, but it's clear only one is used. Emrys pulls a seat out for me, and I sit down in it before he takes the well-used chair. "I can only imagine he wanted to hide them," I tell Emrys. "Maybe to make them unseeable, unreachable. I just don't know. I feel like I'm missing a massive piece of the puzzle, and I can't remember." I lean back in the seat. "Sorry, I know this isn't what you want to hear when you must be worried about your mum and court."

Emrys looks at his books for a moment before he changes his mind and looks right at me. "I have to believe she is safe and my people are hiding. The air is tricky to evade, and we have many, many places to hide in the clouds. I'm hoping for that." He looks back at the books in front of him. Many are in languages I can't read but clearly Emrys can. "I've been looking into anything that can take memories from a person, but there's nothing. There was one book that suggested there were ancient weapons lost from this world that could take memories away, but if they're lost from this world, then they're not here, so they couldn't have been in play twelve years ago."

"What exactly are you looking for in these books?" I question.

Emrys looks away from me, far too quickly. "Various things, like the memories."

I touch his hand. "Why do I get the feeling you're not telling me something?"

Emrys looks at my hand. He turns it over, softly touching the air dragon on my wrist. "Just know, if we don't tell you something, it's to keep you safe. Only ever to keep you safe. We came here for you and chose you. Don't forget that, no matter what comes of us all."

"That almost sounded like a goodbye," I gently reply.

He sadly smiles at me before his eyes lock on a book near me, and he grabs it, flipping it over. "Ah, here, this is what I read about mind speaking. It's a fairy tale from these lands, but the dates suggest it was more than that. It's a story about destined mates. Want to hear it?"

Where have I heard *destined mates* before?

After a second, as Emrys waits for me to reply, I remember Hope claiming Lysander was waiting for his destined mate. "Sure."

Emrys grins and begins to read. "Once there was a bear, bound to a forest and forever waiting for his fate to appear. A woman fell into his forest, injured and near death. Her blood would be scented by the other bears and dangers of the forest, and he couldn't get to her in time. The bear was able to speak into her mind, a gift from the mighty dragon gods for destined mates when they are in great danger. He guided her to him, and he shifted back into a mortal to help the woman, who was his mate. They shared thoughts, desires, and words in their minds forever." Emrys pauses as my heart races. "It's a terrible fairy tale, but there is truth in it. Destined mates are long gone from this world, and the gift of mind sharing along with it."

Emrys keeps talking but the world goes silent for me. Lysander can speak in my mind, and it began when I was drowning. He told me to swim. Lysander is my destined mate, and he made me his enemy.

CHAPTER 13

I make up an excuse for Emrys so I can leave, and I barely even hear the words I said as two words ring in my ears over and over. *Destined mate.* Destined fucking mates. Lysander didn't tell me. The bastard never said a word, and instead, he treated me like shit. I don't want any kind of bond to him.

Fuck no. Not him. Anyone but him.

The camp blurs as I search for Lysander, following that part of me that I felt when I spoke to him. I can find him, and that's how he knew exactly where I was. Emrys and Arden told me Lysander led the way here. To me.

He knew. He knew because he can speak to me

in his mind, and he can sense me. I don't know what god, what dumbass, thought we would make a good couple, but they are wrong. I find him on the edge of the camp, sitting on the ledge of a cliff, peeling an apple with a knife.

For a moment, I just stare at him. My enemy is beautiful in a way that crushes most people who look at him—boy or girl. His red hair is like autumn leaves on fire, bright and cosy. But in most worlds, the most beautiful are the deadliest. His black clothes are filled with his muscular form, yet all of him is tense. I wonder for a second what he is thinking about so intently as he watches the dragons fly.

Knowing Lysander, it's murdering puppies or something just as terrible. Lysander turns, like he knows I'm here. Of course he does. I can barely see through the haze of anger, of denial that this is even happening and denial that he knew—and still broke me.

When he sees me coming towards him, he smirks and stands, tucking the knife away and throwing the apple over the cliff. "Did you miss me that much? Finally realised I'm the better king—"

My hand slams hard into his cheek. He blinks in

surprise. I shove his shoulder as hard as I can, but he barely moves. His eyes bleed with anger and annoyance. Finally, we are on the same page. "What the fuck was that for?"

I go to shove him again, but he grabs my wrist, pulling me hard against his chest and pinning me in place. "No more fucking hitting me. What's your problem, witch?"

I laugh, only deepening his confusion. "Let me go. You total prick. When were you going to tell me?"

"Tell you what?" he demands. "That you're a psychopathic witch? I thought you knew that about yourself."

I glare at him. "No, the truth about us," I snarl the words into his mind.

He pauses, just for a fraction of a second. "What truth?"

Really? He is going to play dumb. Fine. "That you're my destined mate."

He blinks. Once. Twice. But he doesn't say anything as I breathe heavily, well aware how close we are, how I can feel his every breath against my chest, how his heart is now racing. Lysander is silent...and shocked. I can't actually believe that he

157

doesn't know. He stares at me, searching my face like he can find some answer there. "What are you talking about? You are not my destined mate. I would know."

"Liar," I breathe out. "Do you even know how to tell anyone the truth? Or are you just made of spitefulness and anger?"

"If I am just those things, why do you want me, witch?" He leans in. "As fucking badly as I want you."

"I don't want you," I weakly protest. "I didn't make up the destined mate shit to seduce you! Emrys was telling me about a fairy tale, something about some destined mates being able to speak to each other's minds when they're in danger. He claimed that gift was lost to mates centuries ago, but I know it's not." His eyes widen. "It's alive and drowning us both. You knew, you knew this whole time, and yet you still blackmailed me; you still chose revenge over whatever this could have been. How could you do that?" He doesn't answer, so I carry on. "Hope told me that you want your destined mate, that you were never going to settle for anyone but her, and yet you destroyed me. Why would you do that?"

He doesn't let me go; he doesn't answer as we both stare at each other, breathing heavily. I feel almost drunk on him, on his sea scent, on how close he is. My skin feels alive, like a river of water brushing against me in every part of him that is pressed into my body.

"I didn't know." His confession hangs in the air between us. "I was told that I had a destined mate when I was a young boy before I met Hope, before anything, and I never knew that you could speak in each other's minds. I thought it was a strange connection between us, and until you told me you heard me when I healed you, I thought I'd gone fucking insane. When I learnt you were from the Spirit Court, I just assumed that was the reason why. Why I was able to find you, why I can speak in your mind, but if this is true, then you are m—"

I pull the dagger out of my side with my hand that he's not holding, and I hold it straight to his neck before he can stop me. "Don't you dare try to claim any part of me! I'm not yours. You're lying to me; you knew. You're just being a complete asshole about it."

"Trust me, if I knew you were mine—" he starts, walking me backwards, ignoring the dagger completely. I could stop him, one cut and it would be over. He walks us back until we're hidden in the cavern wall, and my back is pinned to it. I shouldn't have let him corner me. "I'd never have fucking let you go, Ellelin. You're mine. You shouldn't have told me. I'm a selfish bastard, and I get what I want."

"You ruined your chance with me. There's no way back from what you did!"

He growls, pushing against me, against the dagger. "Yes, there is, or you'd have hurt me by now."

My breath hitches in my throat as he leans so close, his lips barely touching mine. "Let me go and leave."

"You're going to have to cut me. Stab me," he commands, his voice thick and velvety. His hands move down my body, claiming me with each touch. My hand shakes around the dagger as he slides his hand down inside the front of my trousers, pushing my underwear to the side, and he cups me. He doesn't ask for permission, and he knows I wouldn't say yes—at least out loud. I gasp as he slides his fingers between my folds and pushes two big fingers inside me. "You're fucking soaked for me, goddamn lying witch. You want me too."

A moan escapes my throat as he rubs his thumb around my clit, easily sliding his fingers in and out of me. My head falls back on the rock, and he groans as he continues to fuck me with his fingers. He feels too good, and my body aches for more, but I bite my lip, pulling back the whimper. "Come on your enemy's fingers, Elle. Show me what a good fucking girl you are."

I can't stop myself; I can't stop as my pleasure rockets and I crash, clenching his fingers tight as my orgasm makes my legs shake and my mind blank. The most knee-shaking, damn incredible orgasm rockets through my body, and I don't recognise the sounds coming out of my mouth. I don't lower the dagger as my senses come back and he pulls his hand away. He steps away and puts his fingers in his mouth, licking them clean as he looks at me. I can see he is rock hard, all the considerable length of him. "You look guilty, but you taste as delicious as you felt coming around my hand. What will Arden think?"

"Fuck you," I angrily snarl, straightening my shoulders. "Arden does it better than you."

"And you call me the liar? Maybe we are more alike than I thought. See you around, witch." He walks away, but before he goes, his voice fills my head. "Or should I say destined mate? Or fucking mine?"

I don't have it in me to reply to him, and I bang my head back onto the wall. What the hell have I just done?

CHAPTER 14

Guilt. It's an overwhelming emotion when it comes to relationships. In the heat of the moment with Lysander, I feel like I forget the world exists when I'm with him. I forget that my heart is torn in too many ways, between many kings, and we haven't spoken about Lysander at all. Having more than one boyfriend or lover isn't unheard of on Earth, but it is frowned upon. I never expected to be collecting boyfriends like they are different flavours of Starbucks. They know I hate Lysander, but it's more complicated than that now. I pause, hearing a dragon roar echo above. I look up, my eyes widening when I see Cordelia flying above me on a small black dragon with a blue-tipped tail. I grin as she waves at me, nearly falling off before flying through the cavern. She survived and she has a shadow dragon. The happiness for Cordelia only lasts a moment as my thoughts drift back to Lysander.

I've always thought hate and desire never mix, but the truth is, they mix well. So fucking well. When I was with Lysander, I forgot that being with him hurts Hope, because she's in love with him, and all this guilt threatens to overwhelm me as I get back to the tent. I slam straight into Grayson, and he catches me, holding me at arm's length. "Brat, you nearly knocked us both over." He looks at me, and he frowns. "What's wrong?"

I take his hands off me and head into the tent. "I'm fine, Gray." Other than I just let Lysander, a man I hate, make me come. Grayson doesn't hate Lysander, but I suspect he won't like knowing what happened. Grayson follows me inside, the warmth of the tent warming my cheeks. Before I get to the bathroom and my escape, Grayson throws me over his shoulder and turns us around. "Gray!"

He surprises me that he's letting me touch him this much. He dumps me onto the floor cushions, and he stands over me. "What's happened?" When I don't answer, he takes in a deep breath, and his eyes widen just a fraction. "You and Lysander?"

"I'm sorry." I look away. "Is it that obvious?"

Gray kneels in front of me, turning my face with his rough hands. He leans in, kissing me once. "You don't have to look so guilty. I didn't expect you and him." He rubs his chin. "But we've agreed to share you between the four of us. We don't want to break you by being jealous. Lysander just never said he liked you, but we all suspected he did. It's complicated, it's going to take some work, but we can make it work. Arden and Emrys just want you, like I do."

"I don't get how you can just be so calm about this," I admit. "If any one of you touched another girl, I'd flip out."

"Good thing we only want you then, isn't it?" Grayson smoothly replies, his words ringing with honesty. I have four lovers, four dragon kings as lovers...I really don't know how I'm going to handle them all. The alternative is not having them, and that isn't something I want, so here we are. Gray lets my face go and picks up my hands. "The four of us came here for you, Ellelin. In the Crown Race, we only saw you, and we only wanted you. Lysander never admitted it, but he came for you too."

My heart clenches. "But it's Lysander. He hates everyone."

Gray touches my jaw, tipping my head up. "Maybe not everyone. Tell me why you hate him. What happened?"

It's on the tip of my tongue to tell him everything. About him blackmailing me to make Arden fall for me, only to kill him. Arden comes into the tent, all smiles when he sees me, and I know I can't tell Gray now. Instead, I bite down on my bottom lip and look down, pulling my knees up. Grayson sits on the floor cushion next to me, pulling it over so his arm brushes against mine. "Our girl has had a long day."

Arden moves behind me, wrapping his arms around my waist and tugging me against his chest. Somehow, he instantly makes me feel safe, and I rest against him. "We should do something fun, like drink until we pass out. Our girl became a dragon rider today. It's time to celebrate like we have little time left."

I turn my head. "The last time I got drunk, I barely remember it, except for asking to ride your dragons."

Arden's eyes light up. "The offer to ride us is always there, princess." I whack his chest and he leans down, kissing me deeply. I look at Gray, who is watching, but there is not jealousy this time. This time, he looks thoughtful. Arden pulls us both up. "I'll get Emrys and the drink. Go clean up, princess."

"He's in the library," I tell Arden, who is already at the tent entrance. He puts his thumb up before he leaves. I watch Gray. "It really doesn't bother you to see Arden kiss me?"

Gray rubs his chin. "I was wondering if I tie you up"—vines stretch out of the ground, brushing up my legs, and Gray takes a step closer—"and we both kiss you. I would be between your legs, and he would claim your pretty little mouth. I was thinking about the sounds you'd make as you came on my tongue. Right before I fucked you. I've never fucked anyone, but I've imagined fucking you a million times."

I suck in a breath. Fucking hell, Gray can dirty talk. He doesn't need to have fucked anyone for experience when he talks like this. Gray grins. "Go and shower. I will think over my plan for you…" I clench my legs as he steps towards me. "Unless you want me to take you to that bed over there?"

I swiftly turn around and run to the bathroom, his laugh following me. I'm not ready for Grayson.

He would destroy me, and we both know it. Before I get to the bathroom door, he calls. "Elle, wait a second." He pulls off his shirt, making me blink in surprise. I've never seen him without a shirt on. It takes my breath away for good reason and for a bad. Every inch of his skin on his chest is covered in tiny little scars, over his toned muscle and amazing six-pack. I suspected he was this scarred when he told me, but seeing it is completely different. It hurts my heart that anyone would ever hurt him. It makes me want to burn the world down to find who did this and make sure they suffer. Grayson doesn't seem to pause at my surprise, doesn't seem to acknowledge it. "Wear my shirt after your shower." I take the shirt off him, and it's still warm and smells just like him. "It's not fair that Arden always gets you to wear his."

I'm still silent as I look at his scars one more time before pulling my eyes up to his. "They're my past," he says. "You're my future."

My voice is a whisper, but every word is true. "You're beautiful, Gray. You're my future too."

I could read a million emotions in his eyes as he absorbs my words. I'm half tempted to invite him to join me in a shower. Instead, I grin at him as I go into the bathroom at the back, feeling flushed and ridiculously horny. I strip off my leathers and have a quick shower, washing off the dirt and sand that seems to have stuck to me. Along with Lysander's scent, which is all over me, apparently. Arden didn't comment on it, but he must have scented the same thing as Gray.

I'm such an idiot. Why did I let Lysander do that? Why was it one of the best orgasms that I have ever had? He was wrong about Arden. I don't think it's a competition between both. They both make me feel so intensely alive, more than I ever have done. But it's overwhelming for each of them. There's so many secrets and lies between all of us that I just don't know how we're going to move forward. Sex won't fix it, but it would make me feel better. I just know they would fuck me like gods. Drinking definitely sounds like a good idea.

After towel drying my hair and running my fingers through it to brush it, I slide Grayson's shirt on, which falls well below my knees. I have to tuck up the sleeves so they don't fall over my hands. Thankfully, there's new underwear in here, so I don't have to go out there all commando. By the time I come out, Emrys and Arden are back and laying out boxes with food that smells incredible. Arden also has many bottles, which he lays around the fire in the middle. He looks up at me with his fiery eyes and then over to Gray, who has a new shirt on. Gray smirks. "I found Emrys with food, and we stole the wine from the tsar's tent."

"I'm pretty sure that breaks some rules," I mutter as I head over.

Emrys pops the cork off the bottle and smells it. "Who cares? This is good wine. Not dragon wine, but it will do."

I sit down between Emrys and Arden on the floor cushions, stretching my legs out to the fire, enjoying the heat. Arden's eyes roll down my legs, and I swear I feel every look. He clears his throat. "So, how does it feel to have your own dragon?"

"Similar to how I imagine you guys feel shifting to your dragons. Except I bet I'm going to fall off," I admit. I nearly did on the first flight, more than once. Riding dragons is a lot harder than in theory. It doesn't help that Terrin is so fast, despite his gigantic form. When I rode on Emrys, and even the commander's dragon, they didn't fly as fast as Terrin does.

"It was interesting to fly with the wild dragons when some of them are like us," Emrys admits, offering me a box of food. Inside are cooked chicken, steamed vegetables and rice. All of it smells like it has intense flavours.

"Explain that one?" Arden asks before he drinks from the bottle, then gets his own box, along with Gray and Emrys. They leave a box for Lysander, whenever he plans to turn up. With thoughts of Lysander filling my mind, I grab a spoon and dig into my food. Emrys explains everything that I told him about the shadow dragons.

Grayson takes a long drink and frowns at me. "It's almost like you're fated to come here, and your father knew it. What doesn't make sense to me is why the sorcerer threw you here. Was it a happy accident, or did he know? If he knew, why would he risk it? He clearly wanted the Spirit Court dead and gone. Your parents stopped him for a time, and that means you might be able to do that."

Arden groans. "None of us have answers, and I'm done figuring out this shit without being drunk."

"I agree with that," Grayson states, drinking the bottle Arden offers him.

I sip on my bottle, and the wine is very sweet. Emrys is right, dragon wine is better. After we have all eaten, I curl up to Arden's side, feeling sleepy instead of drunk. The day has finally caught up with me, and all I want to do is sleep. Emrys tugs a blanket over me and picks up my feet onto his lap.

"After all this, do you still want to go back to Earth? To your life there and your grandmother?" I'm caught off guard by Arden's question. He runs his hand through my damp hair. They all seem to watch me for my answer, like it's important to them.

"We have too many problems in this world for me to worry about going back to Earth anymore. I think it's better I don't go back for a while. Plus, I think she lied to me. She lied to me for a long time, and I feel like all anybody ever does is lie to me about the past. I was born here, and I'm beginning to feel like I shouldn't leave yet."

"She protected you and she lost her daughter and son-in-law," Emrys says, his voice soft. "Lying to protect someone isn't an evil act. She must miss you, and we all know you miss her. She is your family."

They might be right, but I don't have it in me to argue the point right now. I lay my head down on Arden's lap, smiling up at him. He keeps running his large fingers through my hair, and I enjoy every second. "You look tired. You should get some sleep."

I yawn and close my eyes. I don't remember

drifting off, but it feels like moments later that I silently stir. I hear them talking quietly. "We should tell her the truth, Arden. We should tell her our plan and how we really got out—"

"No," Arden whispers back, his hand tightening on my hip. "She will do anything to save us, and that isn't fair to her. Our girl will be safe and away from him. That's the end goal we all want."

Lysander agrees with him. "For her."

"You never agreed with this. What changed?" Emrys questions. "Was it whatever happened between you both and why you stink of her?"

Lysander doesn't answer, and I feel Arden pick me up, carrying me over to the bed as I drift back to sleep in his arms. Tomorrow, I begin dragon riding, and I find out what they are lying about.

CHAPTER 15

"Hold on!" Terrin roars into my mind after I slam into his back. Again. "If you fall, again, you might actually hit the sharp rocks, and it would hurt. A lot."

I resist the urge to snap at him that I'm trying my best—even if I'm failing at dragon riding on an epic level. He moves too fast, too sharp, and I always fall off. I don't even scream anymore, so that's a small bonus. My hands are freezing, clutching on to his thorns and the brown leather saddle that's over his back with stirrups to put my feet in. It clips around his neck, and most of the riders have them.

Terrin growls and jumps through a cavern tunnel, swirling through thick shadows and darkness until we shoot out of the other side and into another abandoned cavern. He knows his way around this place effortlessly, but I'm nowhere used to their home. Terrin suddenly flies low around a rock formation before pulling straight up into the air. I hold on until my muscles are screaming at me and my hands are frozen until I can't feel them. Terrin banks to the right, and I fall straight into the air, grabbing onto nothing to stop myself. My stomach turns as I fall fast, and a scream lodges in my throat as I cascade down towards the sharp rocks. I hear Terrin roar my name and swoop down, picking me up in his claws. He drops me on a ledge, a bit too rough. I catch my chin on the stone, tasting my own blood in my mouth. Terrin growls as he lands next to me, a cyclone of dust blowing around us both. "You are my rider, and you can't hold on."

"You're a grumpy asshole dragon who doesn't seem to remember you have a rider!" I shout right back.

He roars at me, shadows wrapping around us both until we are in nothing but darkness. I can still see him, and I know I've upset him. I rub my cut lip. "I'm sorry, I didn't mean that. I'm just frustrated."

Terrin doesn't reply to me for a while, but his

wing touches my back. "I will not let you die, but you are going to get yourself killed if we don't ride correctly."

"How painful is it for one of us to die?" I question. "We share a bond through these marks. Would I feel your death?"

Terrin's voice is softer than usual. "It's painful. It is akin to having a part of your soul ripped from your chest and thrown into the sky to be lost forever, and yet you chase it still."

I watch where I suspect he is in the darkness. "How would you know? Did you have another rider?"

"No." A grumble echoes in the air. "But I have friends who have lost their riders. They are not the same dragon after." There's a pause. "Losing you would be the end for me. I would not recover. I have waited for you my entire life."

I reach out, touching the scales of his wing. That was oddly sweet of my scary ass dragon. "You didn't pick the best rider. Somehow, I always end up in near-death situations."

The darkness bleeds away and I find Terrin right in front of me, his green eyes looking directly into my soul like he has a window that only he can see through. "As long as we are together, no mortal, dragon or god will end your life." He looks away after that vow seems to burn to life between us. "Now we ride, and you do not fall."

"No falling, got it," I mutter. Much easier said than done.

I'm not sure if Terrin hears that internal thought or I accidently said it to him, but he looks up. Three dragons fly through this cavern, and one is familiar. "Your blood bound has learnt well."

Hope and Dalinda are diving through the air around the rock formations, quick and swift, like they have been riding for years and not just the month we have had so far. Their every move is as one. She never falls off. All I can see is her black hair whipping behind her from her ponytail before they both disappear through another tunnel. If Hope can do this, so can I.

Gritting my teeth, I climb myself back into position and lean down, grabbing onto the thorns once more. Terrin takes three big steps before jumping straight into the air, sweeping his wings out to catch our fall. I don't dare do anything but concentrate on him, on moving with him as he swoops around the formations, and he drives up into the shallow tunnel that leads to the desert. The thick, hot, and humid air warms me but not enough to stop my hands freezing after a short time. Everything is going well until he sweeps down, straight into the tunnels, and makes a harsh left with no warning. I can't stop myself as my body flies out of the seat and I fall. Terrin doesn't catch me in time before I slam into a sand-covered rock ledge. I hear a definite crack in the side of my chest as I cry out. "Ellelin!"

I blink through the pain, pushing it down as Terrin finds me. I've definitely broken a rib. "Fuck."

"Are you well?" Terrin sarcastically questions, stretching his dragon tail around me. There is a little concern there, but I can hear how pissed off he is. Right there with you, buddy.

I wince as I sit up. "I'm fine, but you move too fast and without warning me. I know that I've got to learn to hold on, but you need to slow down with the harsh turns. We're never going to get this unless you have cues that I can pick up on and you don't turn into harsh currents of wind that just knock me off."

Dragon flying lessons have been going on for over a month now, a month of this and we are no better, no closer to being a good team. I spend my mornings training with Grayson and Emrys, and my afternoons flying. The mornings are better. Arden and Lysander have been distracted with the tsar, and I haven't seen much of them except for when we all eat together at night. I'm usually so tired that one of them carries me to bed after I fall asleep eating.

At the beginning of the dragon riding, it was easy to make up excuses as to why I couldn't exactly stay on, but now it's getting ridiculous. We don't have time for me not to get this. The kings and the tsar are planning to attack the courts soon with older riders and the tsar's army. I know the kings are waiting for me, or they would have left by now. The kings have been helping to show the tsar weaker points of the courts, where it'd be easy enough to access, along with coded messages to be given to their people so they surrender immediately and don't fight back.

Terrin doesn't reply to me. I've pissed him off once more. I look up at the other riders. They're riding in formations now behind the commander, but until I manage to stay on, I can't join those formations. I'm not the only rider with issues, I remind myself. Livia hasn't got a hold of her dragon riding either, and she swears her dragon throws her off, so she lives with Healer Ainela most days. I spot Cordelia flying with the commander on top of her small dark dragon and smile at her. I sit up, flinching as the pain in my rib flares. Riding back is going to be painful.

Terrin bites out, "Get on. We are done for today, and I have others to speak with. Your people are restless."

"Are you ever going to let me meet them? I have questions." I climb to my feet and walk to his side.

Terrin growls lightly at me. "They are waiting for a powerful Spirit Court princess with a plan on how to save her people and home. We both know you are not ready to be that yet." I know he doesn't mean to be a dick, or maybe he does, but his comment hits home. I'm not what my parents wanted me to be. I'm clueless.

I somehow manage to get on Terrin's back, and surprisingly, Terrin flies smoothly all the way back to camp. He settles on the edge rather than making me climb the steps. "Heal yourself. I do not like your pain. We will try again tomorrow."

I climb off onto the edge, the noise of the camp greeting me. "Great, another day of me feeling sick to my stomach while you throw me off your back. Repeatedly."

Terrin flies off, not without adding his reply. "I do not throw you off my back. We are not as one, and when you open yourself up to the bond, to me, flying will become easier."

"How do I do that?" I shout, but he is gone and only silence echoes down the bond.

I know Lysander's storming towards me before I even turn around. Stupid destined mate senses. His eyes are like a storm on the sea, uncontrollable and full of fury. I've barely seen him for the last month, thankfully, but I swear I see him watching me from the corner of my eye sometimes. I also swear he heals me at night when I'm sleeping. Small cuts and bruises that I get from flying seem to disappear by the morning, and a faint smell of Lysander's scent is always there.

Lysander growls when he gets to me. He places his hands directly on my broken rib. I flinch and grab his upper arm. The pain soon fades away as water, warm and soft, wraps around my ribs under my clothes, mending and healing. "Stop injuring yourself. I don't appreciate the feeling."

I meet his eyes. "Careful now. You are starting to show signs of caring about another person." He looks back at my ribs, gritting his teeth. "You can feel my pain?" Lysander doesn't answer me. "So, if you really piss me off, I can stab my leg and then it's like I'm stabbing you."

He lifts his eyes. "You're a crazy witch, Elle."

I laugh. "Better than a backstabbing traitor, enemy." Lysander takes his hand away the second I'm healed. I don't want to say anything nice to him, but I'm feeling better. "Thank you for healing me."

He walks away before I can say anything else, and I watch him go. Hope walks past me from the steps. "Your lessons are not going well. I saw you fall off. Did it hurt?"

"Would you be happy if I said yes?" I sarcastically question. She looks at where I was staring, at where Lysander has gone, and her eyes harden, like she just remembered that we're not friends, that I'm someone she hates. I blow out a breath. "Can we talk?"

She immediately glowers. "No."

I bite on my tongue before I snap back at her. "I want to explain some things if you'd hear me out for five minutes. We are blood bound and it seems like we aren't getting rid of each other anytime soon. Give me five minutes and then I'll leave you alone."

She pulls off her leather gloves, gloves that I very much wish I had, and tucks them into her pockets. "Fine, but by the fire, I'm freezing." My shoulders drop. I didn't expect her to actually agree to talk to me.

After grabbing some hot tea and sitting on a log in front of a small fire, I clear my throat. "Lysander is my destined mate."

"Bullshit," she slowly says, her mouth dropping open. I didn't expect her to believe me straight away. I can hardly believe it, but the proof is there.

"I didn't choose him, and I don't want him. He isn't a good person, and it's complicated. I honestly think he's a complete asshole, and I cannot see what you see in him other than he is pretty. But that's why he's drawn to me. That's why everything... That's just why. It doesn't excuse him or me, but I never wanted to hurt anyone. I think you're mean to cover up how scared you are and how you don't want to be hurt. I'm admitting to you that I'm fucking terrified and I wish I could be as strong as you are."

She watches me in silence before I continue, "I never set out to hurt you. I don't want to hurt anyone. We got off on the wrong track from the very beginning, and now we're stuck here. It's like Livia said. We are the three left. Well, four, but I don't want to talk about Arty."

Hope looks at the fire. "I knew he wanted you

from the first day. I'd never seen him look at anyone like he did you. I was there when they landed, back from Earth, and Grayson was carrying you. He looked at you in the way I wished he looked at me."

"I'm sorry." There is little more I can say. "They killed my ex-boyfriend because he was going to hurt me. Force himself on me, I'd bet. I'd caught him with my friend, my only friend, and dumped him. You're right, you know, when you said I don't have any friends. Everyone betrays me and I don't see it. Arty was the last one."

"I don't have friends either," she admits. "Maybe Livia, but she only holds onto me because she doesn't want to be alone."

We both look at the fire and say nothing. I'm not sure where to go from here. "I think I loved Lysander because he was the only thing that I ever had since I came here. His mother brought me up, but I was a ward to the court, and I barely saw anyone. They looked after me, but they didn't love me. I thought Lysander would love me if we..." She looks down. "I crave friendship and love too, but I know Lysander doesn't love me. We used each other to fill gaps in our lives and pretended it was more. Lysander found you, and I...didn't."

I go to reply but she keeps talking. "I lied to them all. I told them I have no memories. I do. I'm not from the west, this world. I didn't come from here. I remember being taken through a portal when I was so young. I remember the smell of wolves, so many wolves. I remember my name, but I told them I remembered only my first name—Hope—but that's not true. My last name was Ravensword, and I can see my parents in my dreams sometimes. They are alive and wishing for me," she tells me quietly.

I'm amazed that she's sharing all of this with me, and I don't want to ruin the moment.

"Lysander, he saved my life and looked after me. His mother was broken and lost after Lysander's father died, and I'd spend half the year with her. Lysander brought up his younger brother alone and became a king. He had no choice. The other kings, perhaps, were more babied by the courts, but Lysander wasn't. I didn't want him to be alone. Even when he was bitter and angry over his father's death. That anger warped his personality, changed him to who he is now. He is still a good person, probably one of the best people I know." She sighs. "It was over after that night you got drunk with them. Something changed that next morning. I don't know what it was."

I do. I was nearly beaten to death, and he healed me.

"After that morning, he made it very clear he was not interested. I just couldn't let him go, even when I was being a toxic bitch."

"We can be bitches together." I smile at her. "I would do stupid, crazy things for those kings. Love and desire change people and bring out the darkest parts of us, but hopefully the best parts of us too."

"I can't say we're gonna be friends," she mutters. "I don't think that's even an option, but I don't always hate you and Lysander so much now. Fate has fucked you both over." She smiles slightly. "But thank you for telling me. I think I needed to hear it. The final nail in the coffin so I can move on."

We drink our teas in silence. It feels weird that she doesn't want to stab me. It's progress. "Where'd you get the gloves from?"

She rolls her eyes. "Already asking for a favour." I raise an eyebrow. "The girls' tent, at the front. They have things like gloves and insulation to put in your trousers around your thighs to help stop you from slipping. You can also put chalk on your hands. Makes it easier to hold on."

I stand up. "Thanks."

She stands with me. "One more thing. If you decide to give Lysander a chance, make the bastard work for it. He's still an asshole."

Laughing, I nod. "I promise." Giving Lysander a chance isn't going to happen, because Hope doesn't know the half of how fucked up he is.

I head towards the girls' tent, only for Cordelia to run straight into me. "You're wanted at the commander's tent. Something has happened!"

CHAPTER 16

*C*ordelia stays at my side as we head
through the camp, her arms crossed. Her
curly hair is up in a ponytail, and she is covered in
sand like her dragon dragged her through the desert
today. Even her hair is filled with it. I almost don't
want to ask. "How is riding going?"

She winces. "Not good." Cordelia blows out a
breath. "But we will figure it out. He is my friend."
Oddly, I feel the same way about Terrin. After just
one month, I couldn't imagine a life without him as
my dragon and at my side. It feels like I've known
him forever. It might be because he is from my
court, but deep down, it feels more than that. I touch
my marks on my chest that link us, and even with

some distance between us now, as he rests with the other dragons, he feels with me. "We haven't actually had time to catch up since we began riding. I wanted to thank you. I'm pretty sure I survived because of you."

"Me?" My question rings between us.

She nods once. "Yes. You've been kind to me since the beginning, but it's more than that. My shadow dragon followed Terrin out, wondering why he was coming to the riders. The shadow dragons see Terrin as a leader, and he has always made it clear he didn't want a rider. The shadow dragons don't tend to want to take riders, and mine did not want a rider either. He called it a chain around his neck that would never loosen without chopping it off."

"Very descriptive."

She snorts. "He is like that, my dragon, Nevin." We head around a large tent, which is noisy, before she carries on. "Nevin sensed me and was curious. I was being attacked by a silver dragon. I barely remember anything other than the freezing frost, the white flames that were everywhere as I screamed. I thought he'd come to kill me with the silver one, but Nevin fought the dragon off."

"I'm happy he did." And you didn't die, I don't add.

Cordelia looks up at the cavern, at the dragons flying around. "Nevin picked me up, threw me into the desert. He did not want a rider, but when he picked me up, he had scratched my skin and marked me as his. I don't think he did it on purpose. After spending hours watching me with anger and huffing to himself, he decided that he wanted me as his rider. I made the marks, we began talking, and he explained he doesn't like me, and then he flew back into camp. Seems like I owe you quite a bit. I was ready to die in that cart, and you were kind when no one else was."

I touch her arm and smile. "Be kind to someone else, and that's all I want. Well, actually I would like to know what's going on in this tent before I get there."

Cordelia shrugs. "I don't know much. I was with the healers when the commander came running in, demanding help and telling me to get you to his tent. The healers went with him, and I saw your kings heading into the tent on my way here."

I'm relieved it's not one of the kings that's hurt, but I'm also glad that I'm not going to be in the tent alone with the commander. I've avoided him as much as I can do over the last month. Any time that he even looked like he would suggest we be alone, I made an excuse or managed to get away. I would have made an excuse to leave if I walked in there today and found myself alone with him. He gives me bad vibes and I'm listening to them, although the dragon kings seem to make sure that I'm never alone with him anymore. I don't know whether they're watching him, but one of them always seems to be in the right place at the right time. We stop at the entrance of the tent, and Cordelia leans in. "The girls talk in the camp, and the commander is dangerous. Be safe."

She walks away as the guards step to the side, and I head into the tent, which is a flurry of activity. There's a young man screaming on a table in the middle, screaming in pain. Healer Ainela and two others are standing to the side, talking amongst themselves and holding bowls of something. The commander is standing over the man, and the kings are at the sides of the table. Lysander is holding him down with thick water that wraps around the man's chest and waist, which are ripped to pieces. Lysander stops and the water falls with a splash to the floor. Arden sees me first and offers me his hand, which I happily take as I get to his side.

Healer Ainela meets my eyes and inclines her head.

The commander barks over the man's cries. "Why have you stopped healing him? We need answers and he needs to be alive!"

Lysander looks bored, a hard glaze of indifference over his eyes. Sometimes I wonder if it is a pretence or he really doesn't give a shit about anything or anyone. "Shout at me again, and you drown."

"Ly," Emrys warns.

Lysander tilts his head to the side as he looks at the man. "There is some kind of magic preventing me from healing him, like the healers claimed. The water will not heal him, and he will die soon."

"For fuck's sake!" the commander roars, slamming his hand on the end of the table. The man keeps sobbing, and no one does anything to comfort him. I let go of Arden's hand and step up to the table, touching this man's red hair. He's young, probably only seventeen, and he looks so broken. Blood drops off the table onto the ground, and his skin is paling with every second that passes. He looks up at me, and I take his hand as a tear rolls down my cheek. "Does he have family? Friends? Anyone we could get to be here with him?"

"He is a rider, and his dragon is dead," the commander answers, his voice cold. "I can't remember his name."

"Careful how you speak to her, mortal," Grayson warns, calm but his voice full of venom.

I stare down at the boy, and I don't even know his name. "What's your name?"

The commander speaks over me. "If you can talk, do the right thing and tell me what attacked you. What managed to kill three hundred well-trained dragons and riders that we sent to the court? Tell me what the fuck happened!"

The man's eyes widen in fear, but he never stops looking right at me. Three hundred riders and dragons are dead. My god. The boy's voice is shaky. "A woman stopped us in the Earth Court..." He coughs on his blood, crying still. "She came out of nowhere with red power like blood. We froze, our dragons landed, and I couldn't do anything but stare at her."

I catch Arden's expression—shock and some-thing else. "My dragon is dead. My dragon." He sobs, clutching my hand tighter, and my heart breaks for him. "My dragon was injured in the first wave of her red magic, but our friend took the blow that would have killed us both then. It was like she sang a song, and I couldn't look away from her even when I knew she would kill us. Male or female, dragon or mortal, we all were stuck waiting for her to kill us. She was so beautiful." He says it in a wispy way, like he's in love with this person that has hurt him and killed his dragon. "My dragon got us away, across the waters, before dying just as we hit the shore." A wail rips out of his throat. "My dragon's gone. Gone." He begins to cry louder, his chest rising up and down so fast. "I'm going to die. I don't want to die. I don't want to die. Pleas—"

His hand falls in mine, and his eyes completely drain of any light until he's just looking up at the ceiling. Dead. I gulp, wiping my tears away with the back of my hand before closing his eyes. I never saw anyone die until this year. I had never witnessed death, and now it seems to follow me, haunting me like a nightmare. Seeing someone's life drain from their eyes is horrible. I sink back into Arden's waiting arms, and he wraps his hands around my waist. The commander's eyes are fixed on Arden's hands for a second before he looks away. "You dragons have been lying to us. Who the fuck is this woman?"

Emrys speaks before Arden, Gray or Lysander threaten to kill the commander. "We are unsure, and we did not lie to you. Whoever this new female is, is new to our knowledge."

Healer Ainela moves between us all, covering the unnamed soldier with a white sheet and resting her hand upon his head. I don't hear the words she whispers to the air, not over the sound of the kings and the commander arguing. Arden is quiet, and he kisses the side of my head. The commander barks at us all. "My brother wants you at the front lines to assess this attack, and the new information will need to be told to him. You four should go."

Arden speaks for the first time. "Five, Ellelin comes with us."

The commander's eyes flash with annoyance. "She is not ready to be flying with her dragon at that distance unless you want her dead. She needs to bond with her dragon, and any days lost at this point would be catastrophic for her. My brother will not attack the courts again without your guidance! Three hundred are dead! I'm sure your girlfriend understands this?"

He looks right at me, his voice laced with sarcasm. "She seems more than capable of looking after herself for a single night."

Lysander moves like the night, quiet and unseen, until he is right at the commander's side.

Every drop of water, from the drinks to the small drops leaking in from the roof, turns to ice. "You don't get to tell us what to do. You are nothing, and if you keep telling us what to do with Ellelin, I will remove your tongue for speaking about her."

"Lysander, it's one night," I interrupt, because the commander looks scared, and Lysander doesn't make jokes. I clear my throat. "Come on, let's go back to our tent and talk about it."

The commander watches us go until we are outside. Arden looks over at Lysander. "I didn't expect you to be the one disagreeing with that bastard, Ly."

Lysander only grunts. "I'm still debating freezing his tongue off just to make sure he doesn't speak again."

"We have a shaky alliance with them. The tsar would help the sorcerer slaughter our people if we hurt his only brother," Emrys reminds them.

Grayson grumbles. "What about pulling him into the earth, trapping him down there until I feel like releasing him?"

Lysander grins at Grayson. "With no oxygen, I like it." Grayson nods—worryingly.

Emrys groans. "I don't think either of you

understand what an alliance means. You can't hurt him, or I'd have done it myself already."

When we get inside the tent, Lysander turns on me. "You want to stay here alone with that creep? You know he wants to fuck you? He doesn't seem like the type of guy who takes the answer no well."

I raise an eyebrow. "Like you?"

Lysander growls, stepping closer and lowering his voice. "You never said no. Tell me no, and I'll stop making you come next time."

The bastard won that, and he knows it when I walk away from him with my cheeks burning. Arden looks between us, crossing his arms. "It's your choice, but I would prefer one of us stay with you."

"I'll stay with the girls tonight, and I'll be perfectly safe. It's one night and you'll be back. It's not like you need me there, and the commander was right. I wouldn't make the flight with Terrin yet," I admit. "I need more training."

They look between each other. Arden sighs and comes over. "I'll walk you to the girls' tent."

I touch his arm. "I'll sleep next to Hope. She'll stab anybody that comes in the room for just disturbing her sleep, so it's likely I'm safe there."

Lysander gives me a questioning look. "How did you fix things with Hope?"

"Why, do you want tips?" I hate that some part of me is jealous if he says yes. It's like the jealousy is a storm in my chest when it comes to each of them. I get the feeling it's the same for them too. We have been obsessed with each other from the beginning. Lysander doesn't answer me, leaving the tent.

Emrys is tightening a sword at his back. "Maybe you can talk to her about coming to us and being our friend. We all grew up with her too, and we miss her."

"I will," I promise.

Grayson has packed a bag for me. "My shirt is in there. Wear it."

"Isn't it my night for her to wear my shirt?" Arden protests.

Grayson glares at him. "No. It's my night. I count, you should learn to do that sometime."

Arden playfully throws a fireball at Grayson's chest. Gray brushes it away like it's nothing with a shield of leaves that burn on impact into ash that blows around the room and out the door, thanks to Emrys. Emrys kisses my cheek. "They are always making a mess."

I watch as Arden and Gray joke with each other. "But your powers are amazing."

After they stop messing about, Arden walks me over to the girls' tent and pauses at the entrance door. He tucks some of my loose hair behind my ear. "Don't go near the commander. Don't go anywhere else until we're back in the morning for you."

I wrap my arms around his shoulders, holding my bag at his back. His hands slide down my waist to my ass, and he squeezes me before resting his head against mine. "I won't."

Arden grabs the lower part of my top and pulls my body flush against his. "I love you, princess. I burn for you, and now I've started touching you, I never wanna fucking stop. When you're not so tired from dragon riding, and all this shit is over, I want you under me. I want to know what it feels like to be buried deep in the woman I love."

I resist the urge to clench my legs. "I love you too, Arden." But a small part of me screams that I have to tell him the truth. I'm lying to him still, even as I admit I love him. I've been lying for a long time, and I know he deserves to know about Lysander. I just can't break his heart and tell him.

He kisses me deeply, holding me tight to his

chest like he never wants to let me go. Someone clears their throat, and Arden slowly pulls back, like he wants to enjoy every second, dropping me back on the ground. I search his red eyes. "When you're back, we need to talk about something."

"Anything, princess." He kisses me softly one more time before he turns and walks away.

I watch him go with a smile on my face, and I touch my sore lips. "What are you doing here with that stupid, love-struck look on your face?"

Turning, I see that it was Hope who interrupted me. "The kings have to fly to the tsar tonight, and they want me to sleep here. Safer for me."

"At least you don't snore," she mutters, "or it would be a hard pass on us sharing a room again. Come on, dinner is being served."

My stomach rumbles like it understood her. "I'm starving."

"I heard," she deadpans, and I glare at her head as she walks on ahead.

We collect boxes of food and sit round the fire next to Cordelia and Livia, who are in a deep conversation about how Livia is from Earth. "Earth is like here, but we don't have magic or dragons. People write about them in books, but that's it."

"Do you miss it there?" Cordelia questions.

Livia looks at Hope and me before turning back. She digs her fork into a piece of chicken. "Sometimes. I didn't have to fear for my life over there. I was just living my life. This world makes me tired."

I begin eating my own food, thinking about Cordelia's question. Do I miss Earth? The surprising answer is no. I miss my grandmother, but at the same time, I'm not sure I'm ready to face her and learn she has lied to me. I know she likely has, but for now, pretending it's not real is stopping my heart from being crushed like a bug. Hope finishes her food and looks at me. "Fly with me and Dal tomorrow."

"Why? Would you enjoy seeing me fall off?" I question. Before she can answer, the sound of a loud dragon roar makes me look back over the cliff edge. Four dragons are flying up. My kings. They soon disappear through a tunnel, and part of me wishes I went with them. I clear my throat and look back to Hope.

She smiles in a sinister way. "Oh, I have enjoyed that and would do, but no. Dal wants you to learn, and she keeps going on about helping you. I'm being charitable."

I roll my eyes. A hand falls on my shoulder that makes goose bumps litter my skin. "If you ever want any personal lessons on dragon riding, I would be the best bet to lead you. Make room so I can sit down."

Livia flashes me an apologetic look and moves across so the commander can sit down next to me. He sits close enough for us to touch, and I immediately move closer to Hope. "None of you have any drinks. I'll be the gentleman and get you some."

"I'm fine," I say, but he is already walking towards the station for food and drink.

Hope watches him like prey. "There is something creepy about him."

I nod. "Agreed." Creepy would be an understatement for what he is. I don't like him one bit. The commander comes back over, handing us each a drink. I sip on the sweet water until I've eaten all my food.

The commander tries to make small talk now and then until Hope's had enough. "Right, we are going back to the tent. I need to sleep and so do all the riders."

Hope tugs on my arm, and I stand with her. The commander touches the side of my leg. "Sleep well, Ellelin."

"Night." The commander stays, watching me as we walk back to the tent.

Hope leads me to her room at the back, and Livia goes with Cordelia to share for the night. I barely sit down on Livia's bed before the room starts spinning. Hope sounds groggy and so far away when she says, "I don't feel well…"

I pass out before I can tell her I feel the same.

CHAPTER 17

*S*omeone is screaming at me, but I can't find them. Part of me feels awake but another part of me isn't, and I'm not sure what is real and what's not. There are deep shadows all around me, encasing me in a darkness so empty that it is impossible to make anything out. A male voice shouts at me, urgent and desperate. "Wake up! I'm flying to you, but wake up!"

I'm sure it's Terrin shouting at me through the darkness, but I want to sleep and pretend I can't hear him. I want to block everything out so I can sleep some more. I feel rough hands pulling at me, dragging me awake. An unfamiliar male scent is choking me until it's all I can breathe. Sleep, I need to sleep. "Wake up! He is going to hurt you, my rider. WAKE UP!"

I groggily blink my eyes open, and it's dark, almost so dark that I can't see anything, and I wonder if I'm still dreaming. I reach for Arden or Emrys, who are usually sleeping at my side, but I can't move my hands. It's cold, too cold, to be in bed. I don't remember going to sleep. A dim light nearby softly illuminates the commander's face as he leans down to kiss my neck, tearing at what is left of my clothes. Panic rolls through me as his cold, wet lips press at my neck, sucking and marking. "S-st—"

Disgust rolls through me when I realise he is pulling down my trousers and underwear, and my top is gone, along with my bra. No. This can't be happening. I try to move my body, to make any part of me move, but nothing happens. I can't move. He groans, stroking his hands over my breasts as I feel like being sick. He kneels between my legs, pushing them open and staring down at me as he begins to undo his belt. No. NO! Please no.

Lysander's voice is in the back of my mind. "Elle! What's wrong? I can feel how scared you are. Talk to me. Why is our bond quiet? Why can I barely sense you?" I can't reply to him. I can't reach

Lysander even though I want to beg him to stop this. To save me. He is my enemy, but he would never do this to me, never hurt me. Never take what isn't offered. "We are nearly at the camp. Elle, I'm coming for you."

I can't answer him. Fear clogs my mind as the commander pulls out his hard, small length and strokes himself, looking down at me. "Let's see what makes the dragon kings all fucking weak. I'm tired of them looking down at me and thinking they have everything. Stupid fucks left her."

No, no, no, no. Please, anyone, stop this. Help me. Please. "N-o."

Shadows explode. The tent above us is ripped away, and shadows that are like flames wrap around the commander, tearing into his skin as he is lifted high into the air and off me. Relief soars through me as I see Terrin land with the crumpled tent in his claws under him, letting out a roar that shakes the cavern walls. He looks right at me as screams echo in the air, and shadows that are pitch black and dance like flames stretch high into the air around us and what is left of the commander's tent. No one can see me except Terrin and the screaming commander, but he has other issues. Relief floods me and I sob, still unable to move. Terrin's voice is gentle. "They are returning for you. Are you okay? Did he…"

Terrin can't even say it. I feel like I'm swimming through mud to just reply to him. A numbness washes over me, and I feel powerless, weak, and awful. "N-o. You stopped him. Then-kk you."

It's almost like I can feel Terrin's rage and fury, his disgust and horror like it's my own. The commander is still being ripped to pieces by the shadowflames, and there isn't much left of his dick now. Fucking bastard. Terrin turns on the commander, and his voice is deep, dark, and murderous. The flames dance in the air and they are beautiful, even if they are committing murder. "She is my rider and my destined mate. You're dead. You will die slowly and painfully for touching her. Scream and feel as weak a mortal as you truly are." It feels like hours as Terrin tortures the commander slowly, burning him in the air until he finally dies, and all that is left is skeleton bones that Terrin lets fall to the ground. The commander is dead, but what he almost did will haunt me forever. My dragon comes to me, nudging my arm with his nose. "I wish I could shift back and keep you safe, my mate."

Lysander's voice echoes through my mind. "ELLELIN!"

"They can," I whisper into Terrin's mind as four dragons land in the middle of the shadowflames, Arden's dragon crushing the commander's bones. The shadows don't burn them.

They came for me. Arden shifts back first, his eyes widening in horror as he runs to me. He ignores Terrin and grabs a blanket, throwing it over me and picking me up into his arms. I can't barely move. "What the fuck happened here?"

I swear Terrin talks to them, because the shadowflames burn away and all four of them are looking at the bones on the ground. Lysander, Grayson and Emrys are standing around Arden when I open my eyes next. I can feel Lysander's magic wash over my body, making me feel sleepier. "She has been drugged with something. I'm washing it out of her system now, but I don't know this or how long it takes to heal her. He didn't—I can sense he didn't get that far, and she told me as much."

"The bastard must have drugged her somehow before trying to rape her," Emrys snarls. He is angrier than I've ever seen him. "I was wrong. We should have killed him. We fucked up."

Grayson touches my hand while looking right at Terrin. I can hear Grayson speak in my mind, right to Terrin. "Thank you for stopping him and killing him. We should never have left."

I don't have it in me to disagree with him or Emrys right now. They couldn't have known. I don't even have the strength to wonder how it is possible to hear Grayson in my mind like that. I swear, at one point, I heard all of them in my mind. Arden carries me away with Terrin flying above the camp. The camp is in shambles, and I can't even think of anything as I curl into Arden's chest, into how warm he feels.

I must have passed out, because when I open my eyes again, I'm in Arden's shirt, curled up on Grayson's lap on the bed, with a thick blanket around me. The others are here, all except Lysander. I reach for him mentally. "Where are you?"

"Witch," he breathes out his nickname for me, but instead of the normal way he says it like a curse, this time it makes my heart leap. "I'm not far. He drugged the main water supply, and all the girls were out of it. I'm working with the healers, but I will be back. Are you okay?"

"No," I whisper into his mind. I don't think I've ever been this vulnerable in front of anyone...but I'm not okay. I don't think I can be.

Lysander's voice is gentle, calming. "He is

dead, and you are the strongest woman I know. He won't break you completely. Not even I could do that. If he has broken a little shred of your soul, I will use all the water in the seas to thread you back together. Your soul is mine, and I won't let you break."

I sob out loud, and Grayson looks down, pulling me closer. "Am I okay to hold you? I don't want you scared."

"Don't let me go," I whisper to him. Arden and Emrys look up. They don't say anything, but they are simply there. It's enough.

I search my mind for Terrin. I need to know where he is. "I'm right outside, Ellelin."

"You said I'm your destined mate," I groggily whisper to him. I'm so, so tired. "Was that real?"

"I was born to be yours and wait for you as a dragon." Terrin's calm voice comforts me. "The prophecy spoke of a princess of spirit, bound to each element. In those elements, she will find her destined mates. I am shadow, Arden is fire, Lysander is water, Emrys is air and Grayson is earth. We are your elements, and never again will we fail you. Sleep, my mate. In the morning, we will work on healing and talk more about the truth."

I'm drifting off as I feel Arden stroke my hand,

and Emrys's voice whispers, "I found the book we were looking for, and I have the spell. After tonight..."

"It would be selfish to take more time with her," Grayson quietly whispers back.

But it's Arden's reply that makes my heart pound and my soul burst, forcing me awake. "Sending her home is how we save her from ever being hurt again. This stolen time is over."

Home?

CHAPTER 18

HOPE

"What the fuck happened to Ellelin?" I demand as I stop inside their tent and see her on the bed, out of it. The camp is in an uproar, and people are whispering about drugs and the commander being dead. At least, that's what I woke up hearing. I shouldn't be this bothered about her life and her well-being, but sometimes I find myself actually admiring how strong she is and wishing I was the same. She is annoying as fuck, but right now, she looks tiny and broken on the bed with Grayson.

Lysander follows me into the tent, and he is like a cold shadow. I woke up to him healing me from whatever drug knocked all the girls out and explaining that Elle was in a worse way because of the commander. The fucker drugged us all. I saw what was left of his tent on the way here, and Ellelin's dragon was flying around. The commander suffered, I bet, but I'm not sure what he did.

Ellelin is never this still or silent. I don't know how she wormed her way into being my friend, but seeing her like this makes me want to defend her. I know the kings wouldn't have hurt her. No one answers me. Ellelin looks so tiny curled up between Grayson and Emrys, and the way they look at her... I wish anyone looked at me like that. They look at her like their world starts and ends with her. For them, it possibly does. Maybe they were always waiting for her. Arden is sitting at the end of the bed, his face buried in his hands until all I can see is his dark hair. Eventually he lifts his head, and he looks back at Emrys and nods once. "It's time." Ellelin may look broken, but Arden sounds it.

"Arden, what is going on?" I ask. Emrys strokes Ellelin's cheek before climbing off the bed. "Someone needs to tell me what Lysander brought me here for and what happened to her."

Lysander clears his throat before the asshole tries to speak, and I hold up my hand. "Not you. You don't get to speak around me."

"Hope, not right now. Can you just not do this

now?" Arden demands, sounding tired. It makes me pause. I can't talk to Lysander, not yet, maybe not ever. I'm not sure I'm ready to forgive him, even if she is his destined mate. The feeling of rejection is haunting and swallowing me up. Maybe every orphan feels this way? I've been alone so long, and I chase a dream of a family that I might never get. My dragon is my family now.

I cross my arms. "Fine, but someone needs to tell me what happened? The camps are going crazy —" I pause as Livia opens the tent flap and comes in.

Livia looks awkward. "Someone said that you wanted me." She pauses and looks at Elle. "What's wrong with her?" She runs over to the bed and touches Ellelin's foot. Ellelin might not realise it, but I'm sure Livia is obsessed with her.

Arden clears his throat. "The commander, he tried...to..." He can barely get the words out. "He drugged the water supply to make the camp sleep longer, deeper, but he must have given Ellelin something extra and directly poisoned her when he tried to rape her, so she is still out of it."

Sickness rises in my throat as Livia looks at me in horror, tears filling her eyes. "He is dead, right?

Or I'm going to kill him myself. I knew he was a creepy fucker, but a rapist? The bastard deserves a painful death."

Lysander's voice is nothing but fury. "He's dead, and we heard his screams."

We are all silent, and I finally sense the mood in here now. I'll be here when she wakes up. No more being a bitch. Mostly. Arden looks at me, and his red eyes are drowning, like his flame has gone out. "I sent Lysander to get you both. We're sending you back to Earth, and you're taking Ellelin with you. This world has done nothing but destroy her, and she was nearly... I didn't... We weren't there to keep her safe. We won't be there in the future. Her dragon managed to stop him, but he has agreed she'd be safer on Earth for now, maybe forever. So that's where we're taking her."

I raise an eyebrow, trying to process all of this. "Does she agree with that?" I spread my arms in the air. "Don't answer that, because I know she wouldn't want anything that takes her from you all. The stubborn girl I know would have no interest in leaving. In fact, she would not want to, so don't make this choice for her. We can wait until she wakes up—"

"No, Hope," Emrys gently stops me. Emrys is a good man, kind and dependable, but he never came across to me like he would want to do this to her. She will be heartbroken, and I recently know what that is like. "You don't understand everything, and we aren't going to tell you. Trust us and go with her to Earth. It will be good for you to be with mortals and safe, Hope." He looks down at a weathered, blue leather-bound book in his hands. "I finally found the book on opening portals, and just in time. It's been nearly six months since we got out."

"Six months wasn't enough," Grayson's voice echoes, and there is pain in it. Six months? Why six months? They have always been secretive bastards that kept to themselves, but this is taking it too far.

Emrys is already speaking. "I knew there'd be a book like this. It's going to take some of our magic and weaken us, but put together, we can make a portal big enough to go back to Earth for a very short time. You three are going, and we're closing the portal behind you. No one's coming back or passing between worlds again."

"No!" I snap.

Arden growls. "Do you think we want this? To lose her? I fucking love every inch of that woman, and we haven't had nearly enough time together...

but we don't have a choice. She isn't safe here, and her safety trumps everything."

I look away from him, from how much pain he is in. I can't deal with it. "I want to stay with my dragon."

"There isn't a choice in this matter," Grayson all but growls my way. He picks up Ellelin in his arms as he climbs off the bed. She is wearing a long blue shirt and dark leggings, and a thick cloak is wrapped around her shoulders. She's completely passed out and very pale, stirring in her sleep. Her long black and purple hair falls like a wave off Grayson's arm. He holds her to his chest and kisses her head. Grayson touches no one other than her, and the way that he holds her close is absolutely amazing to me. I never knew what happened to him. I heard Lysander's mum talking once or twice about Grayson's mother being crazy sadistic. What she did was unforgivable, but I don't know the details. I don't know how much was done to him, but the courts know him as the fucked-up king, and there is a reason for that. I imagine the Earth Court never thought there would be a queen or heir with how he is. Now…the courts are under new reins.

"Yes, there is. I'm not leaving my dragon, so I'm staying. Take Ellelin if you want, but I'm not going," I say firmly. I can hear my dragon in the back of my mind. Whatever drug was given to me is dampening my connection to her, making it difficult. I can't even speak to her.

"Hope," Arden begins. I'm used to him being hotheaded, quick, and rash, but right now he is too calm. Like he has broken his soul down and is refusing to put his flame back. "We have to go back to the courts, alone, and we will not be returning. The sorcerer will kill you for being in the Dragon Crown Race, because he sees you as a threat. He had his daughter kill the others for a reason, Hope. Earth is safe for you all."

I watch them all and finally turn on Emrys. I think I finally get it. I knew they had been lying about all of this since they got here, so did Ellelin. "You didn't escape, did you? You were let out. Did you make some kind of deal with the sorcerer?"

"Not with him," Arden answers. "Trust us now, Hope. We have to go. Coming back, it is not an option for us, and we want her safe. We're trusting you with her because we know you. You may be hard-headed, mouthy, and awful to most people, but deep down, you're good. You want a connection, and Ellelin can give you that on Earth. She cares for you; she told us as much. This is for the best."

Livia looks at me. They brought her here because the sorcerer will want her dead too. She looks stunned. Emrys's voice is quiet. "Everything's ready, and there isn't long until midnight. Our deal is over then."

"And our time is up too," Arden admits. "We left to search a nearby settlement for this book because we got desperate for a way to save her from this world. She thought we just left to see the tsar. We would never leave her for something like that. Tell her that. Please. Tell her it was all for her."

"Tell her yourself and don't do this!" I snap. "This isn't right!"

Livia stands. "I know she won't want to go back to Earth. She's completely out of it, and she'll be awake soon. Why can't we wait for her to decide?"

Arden looks at Ellelin. "Because love makes you do the wrong thing for the right reason. She won't leave and she has to."

I cross my arms and head for the door. "I'm not going—" Vines quickly wrap around me, shooting out of the ground. They tighten around my arms and legs within seconds. "Let me go, you absolute bastard!" I scream and scream, but Grayson does nothing, and Livia looks outright terrified.

Emrys lines a circle with red salt. "Concentrate

your power, and I will speak the spell." Lysander, Arden, and Grayson join him, with Ellelin still in Gray's arms. Rays of different elemental colours shine out of their hands, straight into the salt circle as Emrys chants.

Magic laces the air, the taste of it thick as Terrin's voice fills my mind. "Tell her I'm sorry and I want her safe. This world can burn and end, but all that matters is she lives."

A portal blasts out of the circle, a wall of shimmering water spreading to the edges of the tent. On the other side, it looks like a row of small houses all attached together, and it's dark, except for a high lamp hanging over a bench. My heart is racing as I struggle against the vines, shouting for my dragon in my mind and pushing Terrin out. I don't want to hear his excuses. Ellelin will hate him too. Emrys uses the wind to move me across the room to the portal. "Let me go! This is insane. Just stop!"

"No," Lysander states, his voice ending anything I had to say. "You will both be safe on Earth. Go and fucking live your life. You have that option, and we don't. Live, for fuck's sake."

Emrys uses his power to practically throw me through the portal before I can tell Lysander he is a dumbass. I roll across bumpy stones to a stop, lifting my head to see Arden walk through with Ellelin in his arms, and Livia's right behind him. The vines slowly fall away from me, fading into nothing but dust. For some reason, I don't move.

Arden gently puts Ellelin down on a nearby bench. He kisses her head, and even though he whispers, I hear him. "I vowed to keep you safe, even if you hate me for this choice. You are my queen, my love, my soul and destiny. Whatever I face now, the memories of you will feed my soul. Thank you, princess. It has been an honour to be yours."

My breath hitches as he strokes her cheek, and he pulls himself away. "Don't go. There must be a way we can figure it all out if you just talk to us and wait. Whatever deal you made—"

"You never loved Lysander, you know that? Because you were obsessed with him, but that isn't love. You used him for comfort, but I know you didn't love him, because I tell you now what I've learnt. Love means that you'd sacrifice everything, absolutely everything, to make sure that the person you love is safe. It is crushing me, and them, to leave her. Destroying us far more than any deal can do, but she will be safe. She will be home. I love her with every inch of my fucked-up soul, and I've lost so many I loved. She is all I have left, and I'm leaving for her. So don't look at me and judge me for this. We both know she can't be in our world."

"She can, she—"

"Ellelin has no magic, and we soon will be nothing but prisoners. Her dragon cannot save her alone from the sorcerer. Don't you think I've thought of everything?"

"Arden, the portal," Emrys warns.

Arden looks down at me, and he smiles softly. It doesn't reach his eyes. "I want to save you too because you're my family too, Hope. You just never realised it."

"She needs you. She's just been through hell, and she will need—"

"Her grandmother, not us," Arden interrupts with a cold look. "And her friends."

Icy rain begins to pour down from the sky, matching the sound of the echoing sea in the distance. This place looks miserable, and I can't understand why Ellelin wanted to get back here. Then again, she never saw much of Ayiolyn and how beautiful it is. Was. The sorcerer is going to destroy it all, and he has won.

I can't do anything to stop Arden from turning around and walking through the portal. It snaps shut, absorbing the last of the magic away from the street until it's nothing but a damp, cold pathway for me to collapse on. Livia walks over to Ellelin, lifting her feet and sitting on the end of the bench. I cover my face with my hands and silently scream.

CHAPTER 19

I wake up confused. It's cold, rain is dripping down onto me, and it shouldn't be raining. My clothes smell damp with salt water, and every part of my body aches. For a moment, I don't remember what happened, and it's normal. Then it hits me like an earthquake, shaking me to my core and making me hate every inch of me he touched and saw without my permission. The rain doesn't wash it away, and I doubt anything will.

This is the second time this has nearly happened to me, first with my ex-boyfriend, and I couldn't really admit it then that he might have done that to me if the kings hadn't killed him. The commander, even thinking his name makes my stomach roll. There was no doubt what he was going to do to me, and I've never felt so weak. So powerless. I might have been born a princess, but now? I'm human and broken. I reach out for Arden, and I grasp nothing but cold air.

Wait, it's raining? I can hear the sea and the familiar howl of the ocean wind I grew up listening to. I've lost my mind, that's the only explanation for it. A hand pats my bare foot, and I look up to see Livia sitting with my feet on her lap. She is drenched from the rain and lightly shivering. "I wondered if you'd wake soon, it's almost dawn."

I rub my face. "Livia?"

She smiles softly at me. "Yeah, it's me. You're safe and okay. It'd be great if you could share with us which house is yours so we can get out of the rain. Does it always rain here?"

I sit straight up and frown, digging my hands into the soggy wooden bench. This bench has been here for years. I would know; it's on the other side of the street that I lived on. I'm on Earth...but why does it no longer feel like home? How is this possible? I look across to see Hope sitting on the edge of the road, her head buried in her hands. All I can see is her soaked black hair. She looks up and her eyes meet mine. "Are you alright?" she asks.

My voice cracks. "No, I need—" I pause,

feeling strange telling Hope that I want Arden, Grayson and Emrys. I want Lysander nearby too. I need them to feel safe. "Where are they?"

Hope blows out a breath. "In Ayiolyn and we are on Earth. They made a portal."

Livia continues explaining, "That's what King Emrys's been looking for in all the books. They told us they wanted you to be safe. They made a deal, but they wouldn't tell us what or with who. I think they feel guilty for not being there to stop what the commander was going to do to you. I'm so sorry."

"That should never happen to any woman, and it's not your fault," Hope firmly states. "He was a fucked-up, awful creature who tried to take more than just your body, but your confidence and the feeling of being safe. He doesn't get to take that from you, because you're strong, fierce, and even I like you. My friends do not fall, because I'm there."

"I must be going mad if you called me your friend," I mutter, rubbing my face. Everything Hope said is true...even if I can't focus on it right now. All I can think about is the kings and how they left me here, and they wouldn't have done that without being in a lot of trouble. "Can you open a portal back? Do you know how? Because I need to get back to them."

Hope raises both her eyebrows. "I do not know how to open portals, and I'm mortal, remember? You're the princess with powers."

"But I don't have powers, and I'm weak," I all but shout at her. I know it's not her fault, but I can't imagine never seeing the kings again. I can still smell Grayson on my shirt. I can still see Arden kissing me and Emrys holding me. I can still feel Lysander in my mind, even if the bond just feels like a string that has been stretched impossibly far.

I turn and look at my front door, right behind Hope. There's a light burning from the living room and one in the bedroom upstairs. It's so quiet on the street, but it usually is. My whole body is shaking. Not so long ago, I prayed for this. To come home from the Dragon Crown Race and just be left alone. Now it feels like a nightmare, not home. My home is held in the grasp of four kings.

I can't even think about what happened with the commander. I can't process that. Not now. I can't process the fact that I've lost my kings again. This time it was a choice by them. Why would they do that? I don't need protecting. Terrin. I can't feel our bond anymore. My dragon…he is too far away. I push myself to sit up, even when it feels like the worlds are pounding down on me. Why do the kings think I need protecting? What happened could happen to any woman, anywhere, and it wasn't their fault. He is dead, I remind myself, and he can't hurt me.

"Which door?" Livia softly asks. "Your family must be so worried about you."

I cross my arms. "I highly doubt it." I'm more scared to see an old lady than I was to ride a dragon, but maybe she knows how to get me back. My mum must have made portals between these worlds to see my father, so there is a chance. I can't just stay here. I won't. The dragon kings were wrong to put me here to keep me safe. It takes all my strength to climb to my feet and walk to my front door. I knock on the door without thinking on it too much, looking back at Hope and Livia waiting behind me. I thought I'd never get here again, but I'm glad I'm not alone.

Livia clears her throat. "It's your home. You can walk in."

I glance at the handle, thinking about turning it. Livia is right, it was my home, but something feels wrong about just walking in after all this time. "One minute! Who would knock this late? Don't you know us old people need more beauty sleep than others?"

My lips twitch as I hear my grandmother shout, her voice chirpy and happy. Just like she's always been. I step back from the door just as it's pulled open and warm light floods in behind my grandmother. She looks like she always does, a mix of vibrant-coloured clothes and odd jewellery, and messy hair held together by a thin hairband. My quirky grandmother, who brought me up, bursts into tears. "You're alive."

A second passes before she's grabbing me, pulling me into her chest and holding me tight. I hug her back, even with everything I now know. I'm angry at her, but she is my family, and I missed her. I wrap my arms around her tightly too, and for a moment, I let out my breath. A sob threatens its way up my throat, but I refuse to let it out. I refuse to cry. I just keep breathing, even as my hands and body shake. My grandmother leans back. "You've changed, darling. There is too much darkness in your eyes now." She looks me over. "And you're soaking wet. Come in with your new friends, too."

"This is Hope and Livia." I point at them as we head inside. The fire is on and I'm thankful for the warmth, even if I can't feel anything. Hope sits on the sofa, literally dripping water everywhere, and my grandmother winces. She loves that couch.

Livia stands at the side as my grandmother grabs some blankets from the cupboard. My eyes drift to the burn mark on the carpet by the sofa. Finley. Arden was right, he deserved to die.

After my grandmother has piled blankets on us all, she stops in front of me. "I'm so glad you're alive. I was worried—"

I can't hear it anymore. I have to stop her. "Did you lie to me for my entire life?"

My grandmother, who I always thought was the best person in the world, nods. I tug the orange blanket around my shoulders. "Why didn't you tell me who my parents were? An accident? Really? They were murdered, and you lied to me about all of it. I was clueless and thrown into Ayiolyn without any knowledge I was born there."

The tension creases the corner of her eyes. "I wasn't aware the Dragon Crown Race would pick you. It is random, and I planned to tell you everything...but you were stolen from me."

I shake my head, pausing as the stairs creak. I turn, expecting to see our cat walking down, but it's not the cat. It's the dragon kings' mothers. Queen Meredith and Queen Dorothy. They're both together and in my tiny house. Queen Dorothy runs down straight to me, pulling me into a tight hug, and

Queen Meredith goes to Hope. I hear her speaking softly to her, asking if she has seen her children.

"I should have known who you were," Dorothy says, leaning back. "I knew your parents well, and I met you only days after your birth. I should have known you, Ellelin. They gave you another name, but Ellelin was your middle name, and—"

I look over her shoulder at my grandmother. "I have another name? What else isn't real?"

Dorothy lets me go. "There has been much hidden from you, but I have to ask—my son, is he alive?"

"The last I saw Emrys, he was fine. They all were before they dropped me here," I tell her, still looking at my grandmother. Dorothy sobs once in relief and she heads over to sit with Hope. "I don't understand how you are both here."

My grandmother comes closer. "Because they escaped from the sorcerer—Ares. Because I sensed them here on Earth and wanted their help to find you. In turn, I kept them hidden." She doesn't touch me, but her eyes soften. "I knew you were the princess of the Spirit Court, and I hid you from that world for all the years I've been blessed with you." My grandmother takes my hands and leads me to the centre of the room.

"Everyone quiet," she demands. No one would dare speak, anyway. "I knew your father. He was a good man. He used to come to Earth to escape from court life, and he was fascinated with the idea his destined mate was here. He was very good at opening portals, a gift his family were well known for. Your father, Falken, came here once, and he met my daughter in a funny touch of fate. I'd been so protective of her. I never wanted her to have that kind of life of danger that we both knew she was fated for, but they were destined mates." She sighs. "Fate took her on a path I could not stop. We talked about how dangerous it would be for her to go back to that world. I knew what she might face, but she wanted him."

"Destined mates are pure fate and light," Queen Meredith sighs. "It was a pleasure to see their love."

My grandmother's eyes seem to disagree. "She fell pregnant with you on their mating day, and she was so happy. I didn't see her much after your birth. Travelling through portals comes with risks, and it was safer for you to stay there. I never got to see you because I cannot enter Ayiolyn, or I would have come that day and saved my daughter and son-in-mating." Tears fill her eyes. "Sometimes the stars tell me of great changes or danger, and one night they were screaming warnings at me. I could feel a great disturbance between the worlds. It was not a day after your sixth birthday, and a portal opened in the garden. There you were, on your own. You had blood on your nightdress, and you were terrified as the castle played the song of the fifth court to soothe you." She tightens her hands over mine. "You were so tiny, and I knew your parents had let themselves die to save you. I could not sense them anymore. I held out my hand, and you walked to me, even when you barely knew me. I picked you up in my garden, and the portal snapped closed."

I don't remember any of this. I wish I did. I wish I could remember my parents. "Your father knew all of what was going to happen. He warned of the day that nearly all would be lost except for our children. I don't know the answers to why he had this knowledge or how he knew."

My heart pounds as I watch her. "Why didn't you tell me? Why can't I remember this? I can't remember any of Ayiolyn."

My grandmother glows. She literally glows, a bright orange colour. "My real name is Hera, and I'm a goddess. I only took your powers to keep you safe. Your memories of it too. I manipulated your mind. I wanted you to have a normal life, not like

233

your mother. That life got her killed. Your mother had incredible power far before she became a spirit queen. You have all that power too, and you're incredible. I prepared you for this day, just in case, but you don't remember any of it. I'll show you, I'll show you everything, and I'm sorry."

Her voice whispers softly in my head. "I did this all to keep you safe. You are all I have left."

She touches my forehead with her hand, and everything comes back in a flash, memories burning to life like a play that I've seen before but just can't remember. "Remember." Her voice is strong in my head, and I can taste magic in the air, so thick it coats my tongue. The memories come back in little flashes, and I fixate on the ones of my parents. I remember being carried around the court on my dad's big shoulders and my mother cooking with me, and us burning nearly everything.

I remember Arden. The Fire Court was some- where I really wanted to go, but my mum was busy visiting with some local businesses, so my dad took me. We landed on my dad's spirit dragon, which fades away like smoke the second we don't need it anymore. My father talks with the Fire King as Prince Arden looks at me like I'm a ghost. He's taller than me and he grins. "Hello again, princess."

It was the first time he called me princess. Even if I didn't remember. We watched our parents walk away, and then my memories fade to the next one. This time I'm with my grandmother, and I might be seven, possibly eight. There's another person here, a man with dark black hair and eyes of relentless silver. He watches me and he scares me. "Phobos, this is my granddaughter, Ellelin. She has goddess blood, and she needs to learn her powers. You trained her mother. Now help me train her."

Phobos leans back on the wall. "Why do you want me here to help her train? You know much more about it than I."

"You're her uncle and you know my power is of the mind, not physical," my grandmother replies, sounding pissed.

Phobos leans off the wall and walks over to me. He kneels down and looks into my eyes, and for a moment, I see nothing but screaming and horror. "Spirit, that's your real name. They named you after the great line of royals that you descend from. I will guide you, train you, and make sure you can defend yourself when the world you are destined for comes knocking. In return, you will promise me that one day, you will avenge your parents."

"Phobos, she is just a child, and you can't—"

"She is not just a child. She is a powerful princess and the granddaughter of a powerful goddess. She was born to rule and be fucking great at it." He looks right at me. "Isn't that right, Spirit?"

"That's right, but you shouldn't say naughty words. My grandmother will make you put money in a swear jar," I protest.

Phobos grins at me. "Then we will be rich by the time we are done. Now, show me your power."

I step back from my grandmother, years of training and powers and everything flashing before my eyes. My life in the Spirit Court, my parents who deeply loved me, and my grandmother who is a goddess. A fucking Greek goddess. Even our cat is not just a cat. My eyes widen as I remember everything until it feels real, until I'm sure I've not lost my mind. My grandmother waits, and waits, and I don't know what to say to her. A moment ago, I was lost and broken on her doorstep, and now I feel like everything has clicked into place.

I've never been entirely human at all. Phobos, the god of horror and everything fucking scary, trained me from a child. My grandmother protected me, and she kept me safe. She is Hera and trapped here on Earth by Ares. She isn't alone either. I go to say something, but the front door is knocked twice.

All of us turn to it, and I hold my hand up. I'm sure it's some nosy neighbour wondering if we are having a party. I walk over and pull the door open to see Arty. I barely think about it as I reach for my powers, where they have always been, and hold my hand out. Shadows rip out of the ground, out of every inch of darkness around here, and lights go out. I pull her into the room with my shadows and slam her hard against the fireplace, shattering the mirror behind it.

"How the fuck can you do that?" Hope asks, her voice made of pure shock.

I look directly into Arty's eyes as she screams, clawing at the shadows around her neck. "I am the fifth court princess and granddaughter of a goddess. I am never, ever going to be helpless again. You betrayed me! I believed you were my friend, and I saved your life in the tests. I cared about you, and you still helped your father nearly kill me!"

"Please!" Arty cries out, but all I can see is her with her father. Her father who killed my parents and destroyed my home.

"Put her down, Elle." I turn my head back to see Lysander's brother behind me. His mum runs over with a sob, kissing his cheek as he clutches her to his side. He doesn't take his eyes off me. "Please, listen to us."

I look back at Arty. I want to kill her. "Please." The second please from Lysander's brother makes me drop Arty onto the floor. I won't make him beg, even if she doesn't deserve his loyalty. She looks up through her curly hair, and my grandmother watches her as the enemy she is.

"Did you betray my granddaughter? Who are you?"

Arty rubs her throat, and she looks at me in pure fear. "My father is Ares and my mother is Aphrodite. I did betray Elle, but I shouldn't have done. I'm trying to fix it."

"Why do you care? You betrayed all of us, and no one here is going to believe you. Even getting Lysander's brother here is not enough," Hope snarls at her, and she is right.

Arty looks right at me. "Aphrodite has your dragon kings under her spell, and she is hosting a tournament in your castle. The winner gets to marry the dragon kings and rule the courts under my parents. I came to warn you and help you get back."

I straighten my shoulders, my heart pounding. What have they done? "I don't need your help to get

COURT OF DRAGONS AND VOWS

back. I can open a portal on my own and save my kings."

She shakes her head of gold locks. "My mother will kill you. My father will too, but anyone who enters the tournament is promised safety. I will secretly add your name and sneak you in before they notice. There is something else, too." Arty looks at me. "Your mother is alive, and I can show you to her."

KEEP READING HERE WITH BOOK THREE...

AFTERWORD

Thank you for reading! For those who guessed from the hints throughout this book, this is in the same world as Fall Mountain Shifters (Her Wolves) and there will be crossovers in future books. There are five books planned in this series and the next is on pre-order now. Link here. This one is called Court of Dragons and Ashes. From the title, you can guess which court it will be based in.

This book, like all my others, is for my family and for my readers.

ABOUT G. BAILEY

G. Bailey is a USA Today and international bestselling author of books that are filled with everything from dragons to pirates. Plus, fantasy worlds and breath-taking adventures.

G. Bailey is from England and loves rainy days with her family.

(You can find exclusive teasers, random giveaways, and sneak peeks of new books on the way in Bailey's Pack on Facebook or on TikTok— gbaileybooks)

FIND MORE BOOKS BY G. BAILEY ON AMAZON...

LINK HERE.

MORE BOOKS BY G. BAILEY

HER GUARDIANS SERIES

HER FATE SERIES

PROTECTED BY DRAGONS SERIES

LOST TIME ACADEMY SERIES

THE DEMON ACADEMY SERIES

DARK ANGEL ACADEMY SERIES

SHADOWBORN ACADEMY SERIES

DARK FAE PARANORMAL PRISON SERIES

SAVED BY PIRATES SERIES

THE MARKED SERIES

PART I
BONUS READ OF HEIR OF MONSTERS

BONUS READ OF HEIR OF MONSTERS

A monster has stalked me my entire life.

But now I'm hunting him.

My job is to hunt monsters, and I'm damn good at it —until a monster breaks into my apartment in the middle of the night and kidnaps me.

Turns out he isn't just a monster.

He's the Wyern King.

Wyerns, a race feared by everyone, are known to be stronger than the fae who rule my world, and no one has seen them in years until now.

The king needs my help to track down his missing sister from within a city his race is banished from, and I'm the best he can find.

Only, he isn't the only one looking for monsters in Ethereal City.

The Fae Queen's grandson is missing.

Working for fae, monster or not, is risky. Most who are hired end up dead, and I have too much to lose to end up as one of them.

I'm going to find the missing royals and be careful about it, especially with my grumpy boss breathing down my neck and watching my every move.

The Wyern King is cruel, cold, and unbelievably beautiful for a male… and my new enemy.

Heir of Monsters is a full-length paranormal Monster Romance with mature themes. This is a spicy enemies-to-lovers romance and is recommended for 17+.

Monsters are real.

If I needed any more proof than the thing in front of me, then I might be the one going mad in this world. The monster twists its grotesque head back to me, assessing me with its red eyes and mottled skin. It stands at over seven feet, two feet taller than me, and its once mortal-like body is a mixture of wolf and gods know what else. I risk taking my eyes off it for a second to look for my partner, and I catch a flash of red in the darkness behind the monster. I block out the awful stench of the creature and the rattling noise of its bones as it moves while I look for a safe way to take it down without getting us killed.

Clenching my magically blessed dagger in my

hand, I whistle loudly. The monster roars loud enough to shake the derelict walls of the ruins before barrelling for me, each step shaking the ground. Like the dumbass that I am, I don't run but charge right back at it to meet it halfway. This plan better work, or I'm so fired. Or dead. I'm not sure which is worse.

"Calliophe! To your left!"

I barely hear my partner's warning shout before something hard rams into the side of me, shooting me into the air. I crash into the stone wall, all the air leaving my lungs as I roll to the floor and gasp in pain.

That hurt.

Blood fills my mouth as I push myself up and pause as I get a look at the giant cat-like thing in front of me. It might have once been a cat, even an exotic and expensive breed, but now it's been warped and changed like the monster behind it. It might even have been his pet. Once.

It lunges for me, snapping a row of sharp yellow teeth, and I narrowly jump to the side before kicking it with my boot. It hisses as I grapple for my dagger in the dust and slash the air between us as a warning as I crouch down. Its eyes are like yellow puddles of water, and I can see my reflection.

Despite being covered in dust and dirt, my pink eyes glow slightly, and I look tiny in comparison. Even tiny, with a dagger, can be deadly. If the main monster runs, we might not get another chance to catch it for days, so I call to it, "Over here!"

The strange cat hisses once more, and the hair on its back rises. It straightens with its five strange legs that make it almost as tall as a dog.

A pain-filled female grunt echoes to me, and I clench my teeth. "I need a little help over here, Calli! Or I'm singing and screwing us both over!"

Dammit. I'm going to be the one buying the drinks tonight if she sings. Or worse, explaining this messed up mission to our boss. I'd rather buy the whole entire bar drinks and be poor. I jump on the cat, surprising it and slamming my dagger into its throat as it scratches and bites me before it goes still in my arms. I gently lower it to the ground, closing my eyes for a moment. I love animals, but whatever that was, death was a mercy for it. I pull my dagger out of it, yellow sticky blood dripping down my hand as I run across the ruins to Nerelyth. Somehow, she has gotten herself under a large piece of stone barely propped against a wall where she's hiding, and the monster is on top of it, clawing at the gap and nearly squishing her. I see her wave her arm at me from the small gap, and I sigh. There is only one way to capture a monster. Get up close and personal, and hope it doesn't eat me.

Thankfully, with Nerelyth's distraction, the monster's back is to me as I pull out my enchanted rope and let it wrap around my leg as I run across the ruins and close the gap between us, keeping my footsteps silent. Nerelyth's eyes widen when she spots me, but I don't pause as I leap off a fallen ledge and land on the creature's back, grunting at the impact on my swollen ribs, but my dagger easily slides into its back. Its skin is like goo, and I struggle to hold on as it straightens with a roar, but I lasso my rope around its neck with my other hand. The monster almost screams like a mortal as I let go, sliding down the monster's back and landing in a heap on the ground. I crawl backwards as the rope magically wraps itself over and over around the monster until it ties its legs together and it falls to the side. The rope won't kill it, but it will stay locked up like this for hours, depending on how good the enchantment is.

With a grunt, I stand up and wipe the goo off my hands and walk over to where Nerelyth is still hiding. I tilt my head and look down at my partner, who has her eyes closed. "It's sorted now."

Nerelyth is lying face up under the stone, her red hair splayed around her. Her chest is moving fast as she finally opens her eyes and looks over at me, arching an eyebrow. "Thank you. Again," I tell her. "We might have fucked up." I offer her my hand as she brushes the dust off her leather clothes. "Any chance you love me for saving you and you will explain it to the boss?"

"Not a chance," she chuckles as I help her climb out, light shining in from the bright sun hanging over us. We both stop to look over at the monster, who is trying to escape the rope. "Third one this month. Where do you think they are coming from?"

"Not a clue," I mutter, eyeing the monster suspiciously. "I'm not sure M.A.D. even knows where the hybrids are coming from. They still happily send us out with no warning that this wasn't a normal job. Assholes."

She shrugs a slender shoulder, picking out flecks of dust from her flawless waist-length dark red hair that matches the red curls of water marks around her cheek that go all the way down her neck to her back. I'm certain I look much worse than she does, and I'm not even attempting to take my hair out of my braid to fix it. "The money is worth it."

Lie. I've been in the Monster Acquisitions Division, aka M.A.D., for three years, and the pay has never been good compared to the other divisions, and we both know it. Like everyone says, you have to be literally mad to make it in M.A.D. for more than a month.

Most enforcers, like us, are sent here as a punishment for fucking up. I had no choice but to take this job, as it was all I could get with my background, lack of money, and young age when I started at only eighteen. I glance at my partner of just one year and wonder again why a siren is working in one of the shittiest divisions in Ethereal City. Sirens are one of the wealthiest races, and the few I know work at the top of the enforcers. Not at the bottom, like us, which makes me question my friend's motives for being here with me once again. "Drinks tonight?"

"You know it," she says with a friendly smile and tired viridescent green eyes. "I'll send a Flame to get some enforcers down here to take him in. You get back to the office and good luck."

I groan and send a silent prayer to the dragon goddess herself to save me.

I HEAD across the busy market street and look up at the Enforcer Headquarters as I stand on the sidewalk. The streets around me are filled with mortals and supernaturals heading to or from the bustle of the market to buy wares, food or nearly anything they want. The market hill is right at the top of the city, and it's the biggest market in Ethereal City. Fae horses wait by their owners' carts at the side of the main path, and I eye a soft white horse nearby for a moment and admire its shiny coat.

From this point, I can see nearly all of Ethereal City, from the elaborate seven hundred and four skyscrapers right down to the emerald green sea and the circular bay at the bottom of the city. Ethereal City was created over two thousand years ago, and the bay is even older than that. Dozens, if not hundreds, of ships line the ports, and they look like sparkling silver lines on the crystal green sea. Beyond that, the swirling seas of the largest lake in the world stretch all the way to the horizon and far beyond.

Most of Wyvcelm is this land, wrapped around the jeweled seas between Ethereal City and Goldway City on the other side. There are a few islands off the mainland, and one of them I want to go to one day—when I'm rich enough. Junepit City, the pleasure lands. I shake my head, pushing away that dream to focus on the Jeweled Seas, and I think of Nerelyth every time I see it.

The Jeweled Seas are ruled by the Siren King, and no one ever travels through them unless you are a siren, escorted by sirens, or want to die. Nerelyth told me once about how going through the fast, creature-filled rapids and the narrow cliff channels makes it nearly impossible to survive for long unless you know the way and can control the water. Above the sea level is worse as enchanted tornadoes reach high into the sky, swirling constantly over the waters controlled by the sirens themselves. That's why they're one of the richest races in Wyvcelm, because if the sirens didn't control the tornadoes, they would rip into both Ethereal City and Goldway City, ending thousands of lives. But they are not richer than the fae who rule over our lands and pay them to keep us safe.

I turn to my right, looking up at the castle that looms above the entire city. Its black spiraling towers, shining slate roofs and shimmering silver windows make it stand out anywhere that I am in the city. It was made that way, to make sure we always know who is ruling us. The immortal Fae Queen. Our queen lives in that palace and has done

COURT OF DRAGONS AND VOWS

her entire immortal life. Thousands of years, if the history books are right and our longest reigning queen to date. She keeps us safe from the dangers outside the walls of the city, from the Wyern King and his clan of Wyerns who live over in the Forgotten Lands. They are the true monsters of our world.

A cold, salty breeze blows around me, and I shiver as I pull myself from my thoughts and look back up at the building where I go every single day. The Enforcer Headquarters, one of twelve in the city, and they all look the exact same. Symmetrical pillars line the outline of the two-story building that stretches far back. Perfectly trimmed bushes make a square around the bottom floor, and three staircases lead up to the platform outside the enormous main door. All of it is black, from the stone to the bushes, except for the white door, which is always open and always guarded by new junior enforcers. I walk up the hundred and fifty-two steps to the doors, and both the enforcers nod at me, letting me in without needing to check my I.D. I'm sure they have heard of me—and not in a good way. My list of fuckups is a mile long.

I glance at the young enforcer, a woman with cherry red lipstick and black hair, and wonder why she chose to sign up to be an enforcer. I doubt she was like me, fresh out of the foster system and left with no other decent options but this. Many don't want this job, and with the right schooling, they don't have to take it. It's hard work and long hours... and we die a lot. I've been lucky to skirt death myself a few times, and each time, I thank the dragon goddess for saving me. I smile at the junior enforcer and walk into the building, across the shiny black marble floors and up to the receptionist, Wendy, who sits behind a wall of glass and a small, tidy oak desk. I like Wendy, who is part witch, but I don't hold that against her. Her black hair is curled up and pinned into a bun, and she is wearing a long blue skirt and a white chemise top. "Hello, Callio-phe. I missed you yesterday during the quarter term meeting."

"Sorry about that. Monster hunting and all," I say with a genuine smile even if I'm not sorry at all for missing another boring meeting. "Is he in there?"

She nods at the steps by the side of her office that lead up to the only full floor office on the top level. All the rest of us have our offices below his. The boss made sure that he had the only room above when he was transferred here a year ago. Her dark, nearly black eyes flicker nervously. "Upstairs. He's not in a great mood tonight."

"Brilliant," I tightly say and take a deep breath. "Thanks, Wendy. See you around if I survive the boss's bad mood."

"Good luck," she whispers to me before I walk to the stairs and head up to the top level. I'm glad I took the time to quickly get changed into a black tank top and high-waisted black jeans. My pink hair flows around my shoulders to the middle of my back, reminding me that I need a haircut soon.

When I get to the top of the stairs, I pause to look over the gigantic space that I'm rarely invited into, noticing how it smells like him. Masculine, minty and cool, which suits the space he has claimed. Massive floor-to-ceiling windows stretch across the back area, giving magnificent views of the fae castle upon the hill and the rest of the city below it. The towers, the small buildings, the people are easy to see from this vantage point. The sun slowly sets off in the distance, casting cascades of mandarin, lemony yellow and scarlet red light across the tips of buildings and across the shiny black floor. The light spreads across my boots as I walk into the room and finally look over at him. He is sitting at his desk, the single piece of furniture in this whole massive space, and on the desk is a Flame.

Flames are small red gnomes that use flames to travel from one place to another, and in general, are useful pests. The city is full of them, and for a coin, they will send a message for you. I've heard that you can ask the Flames to send anything you want, even death, to another, but it comes with a price only the dragon goddess herself could bear. They are ancient creatures and not to be messed with. I wouldn't dare ask for more than a message, and not many would. The Flame looks back at me with its soulless black eyes, and then he disappears in a flicker of flames, leaving embers bouncing across the desk.

Merrick looks up at me with his gorgeous dark grey eyes, and the room becomes tense. Some would say his eyes are colorless, but I don't think that's true. His eyes are a perfect reflection of any color in the room, and there are others that claim his grey eyes suggest he has angelic blood. Which is laughable. The Angelic Children, a race so rare we hardly ever see them, are said to be endlessly kind.

There's nothing nice or kind about Merrick Night. My boss. His dark brown hair is perfectly gelled into place, not a stray daring to be wrong, and it's much like the expensive black suit, the perfect black tie, flawless white shirt tucked into black trousers he wears, all of it expensive. He doesn't wear the enforcer leathers, magically made material, and he has never explained why.

I stop before his desk and cross my arms.

"Do you want to explain yourself, or should I start, Miss Sprite?"

His deep, cocky, arrogant voice irritates me as we both know he knows what happened—and why. But fine, if we are going to play this game.

I resist the urge to glower at my boss, not wanting to get fired, as I lift my chin. "I'll start, boss. We were told it was a simple monster on the loose on the left side of the city—Yenrtic District. It was suggested that an exiled werewolf had murdered mortals, and they called us to take him in. That was all that we were told, and we went to hunt him as per our job. He might have been part werewolf once, but he wasn't anymore when we found him. He was a hybrid, twisted and changed into something indescribable, but I'm sure we can go take a visit if you wish to see it."

"That won't be necessary, Miss Sprite," he coldly replies, running his eyes over me once.

I grit my teeth. "It was a difficult mission. We

were underprepared for it, and none of the usual tactics for taking down a shifter worked. It went a little wrong from the start, and I do apologize for that."

"A little wrong," he slowly repeats my answer.

Here we go.

He stands up from his desk and walks over to his window. "Come with me."

I reluctantly follow him over, standing at his side as he towers over me. I hate being short at times. "A little wrong is when you make a small mistake that no one notices what you did and it doesn't attract attention. M.A.D. is known for discreetly dealing with supernaturals who have turned into monsters, for the queen. Destroying two buildings would suggest it went very wrong and quite the opposite of what your job stands for."

"Boss—"

"And furthermore, my boss is breathing down my neck to fire you. He is questioning why two of my junior associates have somehow managed to destroy two fucking expensive buildings. Explain it to me. Now, Miss Sprite."

"Technically, the monster destroyed the buildings when it had a tantrum and reacted badly to the enchanted wolfbane," I quietly answer.

"If you were struggling, you should have sent for help," he commands. "Not taken it on yourself with a new enforcer."

"We didn't have time, or it would have escaped and killed more mortals," I sharply reply. "Isn't that the real job? To save lives?"

An awkward silence drifts between us, and I steel my back for his reply. "You're meant to be instructing your partner on how to responsibly take on monsters. What you did today was teach her that you can take on a hybrid, alone, and somehow survive by the skin of your teeth. When she goes out and repeats your lesson alone, she will be hurt. Even die."

Guilt presses down on my chest. "But, boss—"

"Yes, Miss Sprite?" he interrupts, challenging me to say anything but *I'm sorry* with those cold grey eyes of his. When I first met Merrick Night, I thought he was the most beguiling mortal I'd ever met. Then he opened his perfectly shaped lips and made me want to punch him.

I look away first and over the city, the last bits of light dying away over the horizon. "There's been so many of these hybrid creatures recently, all over Wyvcelm. I have contacts in Junepit and Goldway City who told me as much. Where are they coming from? What caused them to be like that?"

"That is classified, Miss Sprite," he coolly replies. Basically, it's well above my pay grade to ask.

"It's probably not safe for everyone to go out in twos on missions like this anymore," I counter.

"Your only defense is that you secured the monster without Miss Mist using her voice," he says with a hint of cool amusement. "That would have been a real fuckup for us all to deal with."

Fuckup would be an understatement. The sirens' most deadly power, among many, is their enchanted voice when they sing the old language of the fae. Instantly, she would lure every male in the entire vicinity towards her, monster or not, and they would bow to her alone. Mortal females like me would be left screaming for the dragon goddess to save us, holding our hands over our ears, begging for death. Her voice stretches for at least two to three miles, and only a full-blooded fae can resist it. I've only heard it once, and personally, I never want to hear it again. I can still hear it now, like an old echo that draws me to her, a flash of the old power of the sirens who used to rule this world before the fae rose to power.

"Am I fired or can I leave, boss?"

He links his fingers, leaning back in the chair, which creaks. "I'm itching to dock your pay for this. But I won't. Not this time. You can go."

"Thank you," I say sarcastically and turn on my heel.

"Miss Sprite?" I stop mid-step and look back at him. "Don't make me regret being lenient on you today. You should know better."

I nod before turning away. "Fucking asshole," I whisper under my breath. He's not supernatural, and I know he can't hear me, and it's not like I can actually call him that to his face. Then I'd be fired for sure. Still, I'm sure I hear him chuckle under his breath.

I rush down the steps and say goodbye to Wendy before leaving the enforcement building and going to the Royal Bank on the other side of the market. I withdraw my day's pay, wincing that it's not nearly as much as I need, but a few hundred coins will sort everything out, and I'll work a double shift at the end of this week so I can eat for the rest of the week.

After making my way through the market and grabbing some dried meats, I head into the complex where my apartment is, listening to the old tower creak and groan in the wind. My apartment is four hundred and seven out of eight hundred flats in the entire building, and it is owned by the Fae Queen, like everything else. I'm lucky I got a place here, in a decent side of town, and it is everything I've worked towards for a very long time. I take the steps two at a time until I get to the hundred level. The corridor is littered with bikes, toys and plants, like every family level.

I knock twice on door one hundred and seven before opening it up with my key and heading inside.

"It's just me," I shout out as I feel how cold it is in here and flick on the magical heating. The weather is always changing so quickly. Some say it's the old gods anger that changes the weather from hot to cold all within a day. I'll pay that bill later, either way. "Louie?"

"Here," Louie shouts back, and I follow his shout to find him in the open-plan kitchen-living area, also where he has a small bed pushed up at the one side. The walls are cracked, the cream paper peeling off, but it's the same in most of the apartments. Louie is sitting on the bed, throwing an orange ball in the air and catching it over and over.

Louie catches the ball one more time before sitting up, brushing locks of his black hair out of his eyes.

"How was school?" I question, leaning against the wall.

"Boring and predictable. Mr. French told me I was too smart for the class and suggested I join the fae army. Again," he tells me, and my heart lurches for a second until I see him chuckle. "I'm not crazy. Obviously."

After the age of ten, any male or female can join the fae army and be trained to fight for the queen, but they have to take the serum. The serum is an enchanted concoction that turns any mortal into a full-blooded fae and forces a bond between whoever takes it and the queen. Meaning that no one who takes the serum can ever betray her. I once thought about joining the fae army myself when things were rough and I was starving, but I will never forget the other foster kids in the homes who died from the serum. Roughly ten percent survive. I will never let Louie take a risk like that. Not even for the riches and security and the promise of power that the Fae Queen offers up.

I'm lost in my thoughts. I don't even notice Louie climb off his bed and come over to me. His eyes are like molten silver, just like his father's were. "You look tired."

"Hello, good to see you, too. How's your mom today?"

"The same," he quietly says, walking past me and opening the door to her bedroom. His mom was once a foster mom of mine, and the only one alive. I look down at her in her bed, her thin body covered in an unnatural blue glow as she lightly hovers off the bedsheets. Five years ago, we were attacked by the monster who has hunted me my entire life. Five years ago, her mate jumped in front of her to save her life, they smashed through a wall, and she hit her head on the edge of a door. My foster dad was the only reason I became an enforcer—because he was one. The Enforcer Guild paid for this apartment and a magically protected sleep until she can be woken, not that we can afford to do that, and the Guild's sympathy only stretched so far.

This was my eleventh foster home, the very last one I went to before I turned sixteen and aged out. I remember coming here, fearful, and meeting Louie, who hugged me. I hadn't been hugged in years, and it shocked me. It was still one of the happiest days of my life.

I go over to her side, stroking her greying red

hair and sighing. I'd do anything to be able to afford to wake her up. For Louie. For me.

I leave three quarters of my wages on the side, and Louie looks down at the money, right as his stomach grumbles. I smile and nod. "Should I go and get something for us?" he asks.

"And for the week. For you," I tell him, ruffling his hair.

"Thank you," he says quietly. "One day, I'm going to be an enforcer like you and pay you back for all these years. I'm going to protect you."

"You're my brother in every way that matters, and family don't owe each other debts like this," I gently tell him. "And with how smart you are, I hope to the goddess you become someone so much better than me."

"Impossible," he says with a grin.

"Be careful on the streets," I warn him as he picks up a few of the coins and shoves them into his faded brown trousers. I need to buy him some new clothes soon, judging from the tears and holes in his blue shirt. One thing I love about Louie is that he never complains, never asks for clothes or for anything that costs money except for food. I wish I could give him more, but I can't.

"The monsters can't catch me, I'm too fast," he exclaims before bolting out of the door.

I chuckle as I sit down in the chair by the side of her bed, picking up her pale hand. "He doesn't have a clue, does he, mom? But he looks so much like dad."

Silence and the gentle hum of the magic surrounding her is my only reply, and I can't even remember what her voice is like anymore. She was my foster mom for a few years, far longer than any of the other ten before her, and she always asked me to call her *mom*. "One day, I'm going to wake you up so you can see Louie growing into a strong man. I'm going to make sure he gets a good job and stays far away from the true dangers of this city."

I hope she can hear me. I hope it gives her some comfort to know I'm here, but a part of me wonders if she would resent me. I'm the reason she is like this. I'm the reason her mate is dead. I close my eyes and blow out a shaky breath. The monster hasn't come back, not for years, and I have no reason to suspect he will now. But if he does, this time, I won't be a helpless child, unable to stop him from murdering my foster parents. I don't know if he killed my biological parents, no one does, but he killed every enforcer family that took me in. I try not to think of it, of all the death that haunted me like he did. My monster, my lurking shadow. I stay with my foster mom for a little longer before cleaning up the house, doing the washing and tidying in her room before Louie gets back, and then we cook dinner together before eating.

"Can I come to yours to play a game of kings?" he asks, referring to the card game we play on quiet nights, especially weekends like today, as I wash up and he dries the plates.

"I'd usually have you over, but I'm meeting Nerelyth for drinks tonight. It's her birthday," I tell him softly. Most kids his age would prefer to play with their friends and have them over, but Louie has never been good at making friends. He keeps to himself.

"Okay," he replies, his voice tinged with sadness. Loneliness. He only has me and his mom, but she can't read him stories, play games and help with the complicated enchantment work he is learning at school. After grabbing my bag, I kiss the top of his head before I leave, closing the door behind me and resting my head back against it, my eyes drooping. I'm so tired and I could use a long nap, not a night of partying for Nerelyth's birthday.

I sigh and push myself off the wall before

heading up to my apartment. It is partially paid for by the Enforcer Guild, one of the half decent things they do for their employees. The night sky glitters like a thousand moons as I get to my floor and look up at the sunroof far above. Three actual moons hang in the sky somewhere, but I can't see them from here, and I wish I could. They say looking at the three moons and making a wish is the only way for the dragon goddess to hear you. I'm sure it's not true, but I still look up sometimes and wish. I shove my key into the lock, wondering if I have any enchanted wine left over from last time Nerelyth came over, and push into my cold apartment. If I get dressed quickly, I might even have time to finish the extremely spicy romance book I was reading last night, on the way to the bar.

"Posy, where are you?" I shout out as I head in. "I bought some of those meat strips you like from the market, as I'm going out tonight with Nerelyth. It's her birthday, remember?"

I've been mostly absent for the last two days and not had much time to spend with Posy—my roommate who happens to be a bat and stuck that way thanks to a witch's curse. I drop my bag on the side and look around in the darkness before sighing. Clicking my fingers, balls of warm white light within small glass spheres flood my apartment with light from where they are attached to the wall. I search around the main area, a small kitchen with two counters, a magical food storage box, and a large worn sofa pressed against the wall. It looks nearly the same as when I moved in, I notice, except for my two bookcases in the corridor leading to the bathroom and bedroom, full of romance books I've collected over the years. My prized possessions.

Escapism at its finest.

"Posy, come on. You can't still be mad at me?" I holler in frustration as I walk into the tiny bathroom, which is empty. "Bats are nocturnal, so I know you're awake and ignoring me, but I don't have time to chase you around this apartment all night."

I hear a small rustling noise from my bedroom, and I smile as I walk over and push the door open.

Clicking my fingers, two lights burn to life above my bed, and I go still. My heart nearly stops because it's not Posy in my bedroom.

There's a monster sitting on my bed.

CHAPTER 2

*L*arge wings.

Grey skin.

Muscular, massive shoulders and thick arms.

"Get the hell out!" I shout, a scream dying in my throat as I take a step away. I pull my dagger out from the clip on my thigh and hold it out between us as I quickly look for Posy, not seeing her anywhere. There's a friggin' monster in my room.

A wave of magic whips into my hand, the sting of it cold and piercing. My dagger flips across the room as I flinch, and it embeds itself in the wall with a thud. The monster doesn't even lift its head. He's... reading—my spicy romance book, of all things—as he sits on my bed. My double bed looks tiny with him sitting there, his dark hair soft and curling down his shoulders.

What the fuck?

My eyes widen as I look at this monster. He's a male. That much I'm sure of, and he's huge. He's sitting in the middle of my bed, reading my book from last night, looking like he's meant to be there. His skin is dark grey and almost velvety. Massive black wings stretch out of his back, but they're pulled in at his sides. Black horns curl out of the top of his thick black hair on his head, and if he wasn't a monster, I might even say he's handsome. He's shirtless, and he has pants on, but a tiny weird part of me focuses on the lack of a shirt for a second. No one looks that good shirtless—except this monster, it seems.

He is so big, and I'm sure he could snap me like a twig. Who the hell is he? What is he? More importantly—why is he in my bedroom?

"This is an interesting book for an innocent doe like you to be reading, Calliophe Maryann Sprite."

I freeze, my heart pounding as his deep, sensual voice fills my room. How does he know my full name?

He looks up at me with hauntingly beautiful amethyst eyes and smirks. "Speechless, Doe?"

"Get the fuck out of my room!" I shout, grabbing the nearest thing on my side table and
throwing it at him. He catches the stuffed purple
teddy bear in his hand, then raises an eyebrow as his
lips twitch with humor.

"Don't run," he purrs.

I glare as I grab the next thing, which is a cheap
statue of the goddess, and I throw that straight at him
instead. The statue crashes into his hand, smashes
into pieces on impact, and he simply sighs in annoyance as he begins to stand. My old bed creaks as I
grab my precious books from the corridor as I back
away and throw them at him as I retreat. He catches
them all like it's a game. I can't hear anything but
my heartbeat, and I can't see anything but those
wings that have haunted me for so many years. My
monster had wings. It's all I can remember of him
before he killed every parent I ever had.

Wings. The beat of wings fills my ears as I burn
with anger. My monster is back to kill me. I turn
and run to the sofa, jumping on it as I pull out the
two daggers I have hidden down on one side and
crouch down in the corner. He casually strolls down
the corridor, and he blocks the way to the only exit
from my apartment as he faces me and crosses his

arms. "Do you really believe that you, a tiny little mortal, will be able to stop me?"

"Come closer. Find out," I taunt. If he is going to kill me, I'm going down with a fight. I haven't survived monsters all these years, my entire life, to die easily at the hands of one.

He laughs, the sound deep and frightening. Arrogant son of a bitc—

I see a flash of black right before Posy flies straight into his face, clawing at him with her tiny, almost purple, bat wings. Posy is only a tiny bat and no more than the size of his hand as he grabs her by the scruff of her neck and holds her up in front of him. She still fights. The more I look at him, I realize he can't be the monster who hunted me. Those purple eyes aren't black, dark and cold like my monster's were. Still, those wings... my monster must be what he is. "What is this thing?" he asks.

I would laugh if he wasn't trying to kill me. Posy yells, "Die, die, die. You supernatural monster! This is my home, and I don't care how horny my roommate is. She is not fucking a monster when I'm living here!"

By the old gods. My cheeks burn.

The monster smirks and looks over at me. "You have a talking bat."

"Let her go!" I demand as I look between them and the door. I don't know how I will make it to the door to run if I go for Posy.

He sighs, and Posy is still ranting away, unaware that no one is listening to her anymore. Or the fact this monster isn't my date and that he is here to kill me. "No. We are leaving."

"We are not," I say at the same time Posy declares, "Finally. Go to the monster's place and do the dirty. Between keeping me here as your pet and your new fuck buddy, I think you have a weird thing for bats."

"We bats can be very fun," the monster agrees with a hint of dry amusement that makes him seem almost mortal. Almost. He is very much not.

He lets Posy go, and she flies into my bedroom, slamming the door shut. I need a better room-mate/pet. Posy sucks.

"Then go and have fun somewhere else, or I'm going to pin those nice wings of yours to my wall," I say, holding the daggers up higher. Why he hasn't used his magic to rid me of them yet floats into the back of my mind. Maybe he is playing with me. "What are you, anyway?"

"Wyern," he coolly answers. "Haven't you seen any in your career?"

No, I haven't, or I'd be very dead. My blood runs cold as I take him in, a Wyern male, in my living room. The Wyerns are immortal, deadly, and everyone knows they are forbidden from entering Ethereal City. Some say they are fae—an old race of them. Some say they were created by the fae and are born monsters.

I should have known he's not a monster. Not exactly, but not far from one. From what I know, the Wyerns live in the Forgotten Lands, a punishment from my queen for the war they started thousands of years ago. Some say the sirens siding with the Fae Queen was the only way we won.

One trained Wyern male can slaughter ten trained fae in minutes.

My heart races as I take all of this in. If I call for help and they find me here with him, even if he is trying to kill me or take me somewhere, the queen will execute me for treason. "If the queen finds you here, which she will, we are both dead. Leave."

He steps towards me, an amused smirk on his lips. "Your precious queen would be very honored if I turned up in her city, but perhaps a little angry I came for you and not to see her."

"What?"

He glowers at me. "Are you mortals truly this dense? We. Are. Leaving."

"We certainly are not going anywhere!"

He takes another step forward, and I start to back away until the back of my knees touch the sofa.

I lash out at him with my daggers, cutting through his arm, and it bubbles with blood. He doesn't even notice as he grabs my hands, squeezing tight enough I'm forced to drop the daggers with a yelp. I kick at his shin, which is like a rock and only hurts me, and he grabs me by the waist and throws me over his shoulder like I weigh nothing. I scream and kick him in the stomach and slam my hands on his solid back, but nothing makes his arm shift from his iron tight grip on me.

Magic wraps around me firmly, its icy sting burning into my skin, and I hiss in pain as my head spins. I hate magic.

"Let me go!" I scream over and over. He only laughs like it's deeply amusing to him as he walks out of my apartment by kicking my front door open. I look up in horror as he spreads his massive wings out, and magic lashes around us as he shoots up the flights of stairs. The stairs whip up around us as I scream, ducking my head as my stomach feels like a million butterflies have burst to life. He crashes through the glass, bits of it cutting into my arms, and launches us into the night sky above the city. His wings beat near my face, and I stop trying to fight him. If he drops me, I'm dead.

It doesn't stop the lash of magic that slams into my head and knocks me out cold seconds later, leaving me dreaming of wings and star-filled night skies.

CHAPTER 3

" *ake her, Vivienne. Just take her and run!"*

I snuggle down into my bed, clutching the sheets tighter as I hear crashing noises, shouting and doors slamming. It's happening again. He has come for me again. No, no, no...

"We both can run and fight him," my foster mom pleads. I've only been here a year. It's too soon for the monster to come for me.

"No. She needs someone to live for her," my foster dad exclaims, and the door to my room slams. "She is just six years old, and all she has known is death. Someone has to tell her why, someone has to explain the truth."

"He'll never stop," Vivienne cries. "We

286

shouldn't have taken her in after—"

"I have no regrets. We do this for the Guild. For our queen and what she gave," he interrupts her. Hands pull my quilt back, and I look up at my foster dad with panicked eyes. His voice is gentle and as soft as his brown eyes as he stares down at me. "You need to go with Vivienne and run. It's here, and I'm going to stop it."

"But—"

He hushes me, kissing my forehead. "It's been an honor to care for you, Calliophe Maryann Sprite. Live."

I gulp, tears falling down my cheeks as Vivienne picks me up, holding me to her. She always picks me up, telling me how small I am for my age, and I cling to her neck, wishing this is all a dream. It's not real. The monster isn't real.

I hide my head in her bright red hair, peeping out to look at my foster dad standing by the door. He looks over his shoulder, holding a silver sword in front of him, an enchanted rope dangling from his fingers. "Live for all of us, Calliophe."

Vivienne and he share a look for a moment before she carries me to the window, and my foster dad opens the door, shutting it behind us. Vivienne opens the window before sitting on the edge, the icy wind blowing around us, snowflakes littering the air. My breath comes out like smoke as I shiver. "Hold on to me and don't let go."

I nod against her shoulder as she jumps off the window ledge into the snowy night, and I cling to her as she lands in a thump on the ground. Vivienne wraps her arms around me before she sprints across the grass, leaping over the small brown fence and past the swing tied to the old oak tree. I keep looking over her shoulder for the monster inside my home, but no lights are on, and there is nothing but the glittering night sky until I hear a male scream.

Vivienne stops and slowly turns back, holding me tightly to her. She puts me down on the ground and points at the woods a few feet away. "I have to go back for him. I love him. You have to run. Don't stop running. Find someone, anyone, and tell them to call the Guild. Tell them we're in trouble, but you need to run."

"I don't want to be on my own," I wail as she lowers me to the ground, pulling my arms from her and stepping back.

She kisses my forehead. "I'm so sorry, but he is all I have."

"You have me."

I try to catch her hand, but she pushes me away

before she runs back to the house. Tears fall down my cheeks, and I shake from head to toe as I turn and run into the tall, dark trees. I cling to the nearest tree, the bark scratching my hands and the branches snatching in my hair. Everything is silent for a moment before I hear Vivienne scream and cry out, and then there is silence once more. I hear a door being smashed open, and I turn to see a male stepping out into the shadows. He has gigantic wings that spread out like shadows in the night, but I can't see anything else as he turns my way.

Terrified, I run deep into the forest, letting it swallow me in its darkness.

I wake up with my heart racing fast in my chest as I blink and look around, tasting the icy sting of magic on my tongue. It was just a dream. I click my fingers, and lights burn up in the room, and I go still.

It wasn't a dream.

I've been kidnapped by that arrogant, and a little beautiful, monster. The bat guy. Shit. I take in the scents around me on the soft sheets, and I frown. Masculine. This is that monster's bedroom. By the goddess. I push the dark midnight blue sheets off me, noticing my boots are missing as I look at the bedroom. Expensive and exotic wood makes the massive bed I'm on, and there are matching wardrobes and a dresser. They go well with the dark red walls and polished oak beams that run across the ceiling and the carmine curtains. I look back at the headboard, which is one magnificent piece of wood carved and polished.

My legs are shaky from the magic and a little fear as I walk across the hardwood floors and to the window. The window is massive, ceiling to floor, with black squares all over it. My heart stops as I look outside at the unfamiliar mountains.

We aren't in Ethereal City.

If I had to guess where I am... The Wyern are said to live in the Forgotten City, in the thick mountains to the north of Ethereal City. I've only ever seen these mountains from a far distance, and then they were nothing more than a dot on the horizon. Now, I'm in the middle of them. The mountains are steep, covered in jagged spikes and snow. It's kind of pretty, with the night sky hanging behind, the sun slowly rising.

I think it's safe to bet I'm not going to work today.

My heart is still racing, and I will myself to calm down. If the Wyern wanted me dead, I would be dead. No, he must want me for something else, and that gives me time to make a plan and escape.

Somehow.

I glance around to see if I can find anything useful to defend myself, but there isn't much, just a dresser, two wardrobes, and a rug. I search the wardrobe and drawers, finding male clothes and nothing else. Unless I plan to throw socks at him, my search isn't going well. I find my boots by the end of the bed and slide them on, finding the two small knives I hid in the heel have been taken. My mouth feels dry as I go to the dark wooden double doors and test the silver handles to see if I'm locked in. The doors click open to my surprise, and I peek out into the corridor. The same dark wood floor stretches down a long and wide passageway, and there's a dark red, patterned runner running down the entire length of it. There are endless doors on either side and more light orbs lighting up the space on the ceiling. I hear vague scuffling, voices and music from the left side, and the right is completely empty and silent but a dead end by the looks of it.

I quietly shut the door behind me as I step out and head down the passageway, wishing I had some of my weapons on me. I try a few handles on my way, but all of them are locked, to my annoyance.

I blow out a shaky breath when I see a door open a few feet away, the noise coming from in there and orange light shining out the gap. My hair falls around my shoulders, and I tuck a strand behind my ear as I follow the sounds of the music. It's old music, but it's sensual and soft and not what I expect to hear. I walk the final steps to the door and peek into the massive room. Pillars and tapestries line the walls, all of it old and stunning, and the soft music is being played by magic throughout the air, the taste of it coating my tongue. Several cushioned areas lie around three giant waterfalls with statues of the goddess in the center of them, water pouring out of her hands. The room is warm and cozy, but maybe not the people inside it. Wyerns. Each one of them looks slightly different, all dark or grey skinned, and there are at least twenty female mortals in here with them. By the moans, they're clearly having fun, and I try not to look too long at any one of them. They are all having sex.

Except a few. Like the male on the seating area nearest me. He is different from the others; his light grey skin is littered with small and large scars, and his horns have been cut off. He doesn't have wings, and his eyes are a soft forest green as he looks my way. He has a grey shirt on that a female with long brown hair is pawing at. In fact, he has three females lying on his lap, and one of them is stroking him underneath his trousers. He still watches me, tilting his head to the side with a little smirk on his lips as one of the other females runs her hand through his short brown hair. Dear god, I just walked into a monster orgy. Absolutely brilliant. I really hope that is not what they brought me here for. I haven't had sex with anyone for over two years thanks to my work. And even then, I prefer a heated few hours at their place and then I disappear. I don't do long-term anything.

I'm certainly not staying here if this is the plan.

"The doe is awake," the male shouts, and many male laughs follow. Fuck it.

I push the door open and head inside, letting the door slam against the wall. "Kidnapping is illegal. I'm leaving if one of you will be kind enough to show me the door."

"I don't think so, little doe," the male says, gently pushing the females off him and standing. He walks up to me, towering over me. "We've been waiting for you to wake up. Do you want a drink?"

I glower at him. "No."

"Come on, relax. Have you never seen a royal court having fun before?"

"This is a royal court?" I say dryly. "Looks more like—"

"Ah, be nice. You don't insult someone's home when you're a guest," he interrupts.

"I'm not a guest. I didn't come here willingly!" I protest.

"Still, be nice, little mortal."

He pats me on the head and looks back at the beautiful females on the sofa, who giggle. By the goddess. It stinks of sex in here, and the moans are getting louder than the music. "No."

"How about that drink?"

"No," I repeat, and he smiles at me. "I want to know why I'm here? Where's the male that kidnapped me and took me?"

He sighs, stepping closer, and offers me his hand. He smells of wine and bad decisions. Nerelyth would love him. "My name is Lorenzo Eveningstar."

I don't take it, considering what he has just been doing, and raise an eyebrow. He chuckles deep and low. "Usually when someone tells you their name, you shake their hand and tell them your name. Do mortals like yourself no longer know manners?"

"So you don't know my name? After kidnapping me—"

"I didn't kidnap you," he quickly corrects me.

I rub my forehead. "My name is Calliophe."

"Ah, I did wonder if it was Doe," he smiles and looks me over. "I don't know what my king is thinking."

King?

The Wyern King kidnapped me?

By the goddess, I'm dead. I'm so dead.

I cross my arms with bravado I don't have. "Why am I here, Lorenzo?"

"I believe that is for King Emerson Eveningstar to answer," another voice answers.

I turn to look over at the female walking towards me. She's fae. This female is a full-blooded fae. She's wearing pretty much nothing but a slip of silver sheer fabric that makes up a dress that is wrapped around her large breasts and thin waist before falling to her feet. She is flawless. Fae always are. Everything about them is designed to trick mortals like myself into trusting them. Her beautiful silvery blonde hair that is loosely held up, curls and falls around her shoulders and slender face. She stops in front of me, and her eyes light up in different shades of purple and blue.

Lorenzo smiles at the fae female. "Calliophe, meet another member of our court, Zurine Quarzlin. Rine, she is looking for Emerson."

Zurine looks me over from the top of my head to my feet, focusing on my eyes for a second. I search her eyes and see nothing but sadness hidden within them. "Why don't I show you the way?"

My smile is tight. "Alright."

She waves her hand at the door, and I follow her through, glancing back to see Lorenzo swaggering back to the females. "I imagine you're confused and worried, but ignore the males here. As usual, they think with their cocks and not their minds half the time, much like the rest of our court. That's not why he brought you here. The mortal females come to our court willingly for the pleasure."

I dryly chuckle. "Confused? I was kidnapped by a monster."

"My king isn't a monster," she says softly, her voice full of affection. "Even if he appears as one."

"I hadn't seen a Wyern before, so to me, he looked like one. Then he kidnapped me...," I drawl.

She laughs lightly as we head down the corridor, and our conversation drifts off until I need to fill the silence instead of feeling so nervous. "I haven't seen many fae before. Only one or two. Most don't come down to the lower parts of Ethereal City, and my work doesn't lead me anywhere near the castle or the fae district."

She doesn't look down at me. "Then you are lucky, mortal."

"Perhaps," I mutter. "So you're part of this court even when you're not one of them?"

She looks at me this time as we go through a door and into a corridor with long windows on each side. "Yes, and for what it is worth, you can trust me. You won't be able to trust many here."

One of these Wyerns is my monster, hunted me from birth, and I won't trust anyone here until I find who it is. And kill them.

"For what it's worth, I don't believe trusting anyone here is going to end with anything but my death."

She smiles at that. "You're a smart mortal."

Weird compliment.

"Although you're not all mortal, are you? You definitely have a bit of fae in your bloodline with those eyes. Who was it?"

I look at the shiny floor. "I don't know any of my family."

"Oh, I'm sorry. Is your hair natural or enchanted?"

"Enchanted by a dodgy spell, and I haven't been able to change it back since I was fifteen," I explain with a chuckle. "It was a lesson in why you don't buy enchantments from strangers on the market."

She laughs. "I think pink is your color."

I smile for a moment at the fae female. "Thank you."

She leads me down several corridors, through a few more empty rooms, each more confusing than the last until I'm thoroughly lost. We both stay silent until we come to a massive pair of imposing doors at the end of a corridor. These are curved to almost look like bat wings, and they are old, much like the walls around it. Zurine pulls the doors open and moves to the side. "I'll leave you to him. Remember, with these males, they will bite if you push too much."

She lowers her voice. "But most of them have a soft heart underneath it all. Especially the king."

I walk into the gigantic room, eyeing the red carpet that runs up to a platform at the back of the room, where a king sits on a massive throne. The throne is made of black oak, with five long spikes making the headboard that looks like the spiked mountains outside. The throne room, which I'm guessing this is, is magnificent. Pillars line the walls with windows between them, lined with black squares. Fae light, a rare and expensive form of magic, hovers in tiny little stars across the entire ceiling, and it makes it look like the endless night sky.

Beautiful and daunting.

I turn my gaze to the throne, pulled towards it with an invisible tug deep in my chest.

The king sits on his throne, his legs spread wide, his wings hanging off the sides of the seat. Tight black leathers spread across his chest and down his arms, and into his leather trousers. The shine of the leather reminds me that they must be enchanted, maybe by himself. I'm not sure what powers the Wyerns have, but if they can effortlessly fight the fae, making enchantments should be nothing. His hand is dug into the brown hair of a female between his knees, her head resting on his knee. The room smells of sex, and looking at the pair of them, it's clear what they have been doing. The female doesn't even look at me as she stares up at Emerson, and he tilts his head to the side as his eyes lock on mine. The move is pure predator-like with a stillness only an immortal can have. "What do you want?"

I shiver from his deep, cold voice, but I don't

cower. "That's the very question I came to ask you. Considering you kidnapped me."

He stands up off his throne with fury in his eyes, leaving the female on her knees, and walks towards me with a casualness that makes me fear him. He is so tall I have to arch my neck to look at him as he stops close. "Mortals bow to kings. Get on your knees."

"No," I bite out.

A lash of magic slams into my knees, and I fall to my knees before the king, unwillingly, and I glare at him as his magic surrounds me, holding me in place.

He looks down at me like I'm a bug to a bird flying high above. To him, I might as well be. "Next time I tell you to bow, you bow. Next time I tell you anything, you do it. Welcome to my court, Doe. Stay here."

He walks past me, leaving me locked in his magic as the mortal female rushes past me to follow him out. Only when the throne room doors slam shut behind me does the magic fade away, and I bite back the urge to scream.

I really, really hate the king.

CHAPTER 4

I slam my fists repeatedly against the throne room doors in frustration. "Let me out! Let me out!"

The doors don't budge, neither do the handles, which feel like ice to touch. Magic.

I scream in frustration, but no one comes for me, and I swear I hear a male laugh on the other side of the door. Eventually, I give up when my hands start to hurt, and back away from the door.

Wrapping my arms around myself, I look around the room before walking over to the windows. Wherever this is inside the castle, it's definitely at the highest point or near it. The mountain spikes look lower, and I know if I jumped out this window somehow, I'd impale myself on one of

301

them. Birds duck and dive through the air on the breeze, dancing to an invisible element, and I watch them for a long time until they disappear into the black mountains.

The sun is shining high in the sky, climbing with every hour that passes as I stay locked in here. My stomach is rumbling and my mouth is dry when the doors finally open, and I climb up off the floor. I cautiously watch as Lorenzo walks in, followed by four Wolven males. I recognize some of them from the first room I saw, but now they have clothes on at least. Lorenzo flashes me a toothy smile, and I glare at him as Zurine wanders in after them. She walks my way, smiling softly at me.

I cross my arms. "He locked me in here."

"He's not in the best of moods today," she tells me gently with amusement in her eyes. "Seems you've riled him up."

"It wasn't me. It looked like he was in a foul mood well before he kidnapped me and locked me in here."

"You will understand why you're here in a moment. We're about to have a court meeting, and you're invited as a guest," she kindly tells me, waving in the direction the others went. "Please, come and sit with me."

I do not have a choice, and we both know it. I reluctantly follow her behind the throne room where there is a large circular slate table and brown leather, backless stools spread around it. Lorenzo and the others are talking quietly by the side of the table, and they go silent when we get close.

Zurine takes a seat, and I sit down next to her, crossing my legs and resting my hands on them to stop them from shaking. Lorenzo comes and sits next to me, close enough his arm brushes my arm, and I move away.

The four other Wyerns take some of the remaining seats while we wait for the king, and I feel them all staring at me as I keep my eyes straight ahead.

"Let me do some introductions. Everyone, this is Calliophe Maryann Sprite. She's a mortal who works at Monster Activities Division of the Enforcer Guild and is considered one of the best they have," Lorenzo states.

I turn to look at him. "Someone's been doing their homework."

"Only when young, beautiful mortals are the research topic," he replies with a flirty tone.

"Charming, but don't waste your flirting skills on me. I'm sure there are other poor mortals for you to bless," I coolly reply, because he is charming, and good looking, but he is one of them. I've never been good at flirting, and as Nerelyth tells me, I don't need to flirt when I'm pretty and want nothing long-term with anyone. Long-term means there is a risk of my monster coming and killing them. I can't have the happy ending, the family and one true love. I've been on four dates, had three lovers, and that has been enough. Still, I can see why willing mortals wish to come here and be with them. The Wyerns remind me of the male fae: beautiful, alluring, and likely much better in bed than mortal males.

One of the other Wyerns chuckles low. "She has you sussed, Lorz."

This one is shorter than the others as I turn to face him. His wings are near pitch black and tall, and his skin is a similar tone. His eyes are like melted honey as he looks over at me and warmly smiles. His head is completely shaven, and three silver earrings are clipped to the tip of his left ear. "I'm Felix Masterlight. This is my brother, Nathiel. It's a pleasure."

His voice is like honey, too. His brother looks nearly identical. So much so, I would say they might be twins. Nathiel doesn't smile at me, but he simply inclines his head.

I nod mine back. "I would say it's nice to meet you, but..."

One of the Wyerns on the other side of the table coolly chuckles. "You've been kidnapped and dragged here, and you believe we are monsters."

I look over at the male who spoke, his voice gruff and playful, and the fourth court member. These Wyerns look like the opposite of each other. The one who spoke has dirty blond hair that hasn't been brushed and falls down to his ears, and he has more of a slim build. The male next to him has jet black hair, is more muscular than even the king, and his face is littered with small scars. He scowls at me, and it doesn't faze me like it would do most people. I face monsters every day.

"You're right, Ferris. I don't believe she likes us," the scowling one says.

The blond runs his eyes over me. "I'm sure I could find a way to encourage her to like us."

"Mortals are a waste of everyone's time unless they are on their knees. Begging," the other male coolly states to his brother, not even bothering to look at me.

Ferris laughs low. "True, Julian. True."

Bastards.

We sit in silence for a while, the silence getting more and more daunting, until I hear the doors slam open and his footsteps echo across the floor. He storms into the throne room, and I twist my neck to watch as he walks in, past me and around the table, before taking a seat.

Everyone bows their head once, and he looks directly across at me when I don't bow mine.

He may have forced me to my knees, but I won't willingly ever bow to him.

I look away first, needing to or it's hard to breathe, and find Zurine carefully watching me.

"We're going to make it simple for you to understand," King Emerson begins, his tone bored. "I brought you here—"

"Kidnapped," I correct.

"Don't interrupt the king," Julian growls at me, making the hair on my arms spike up.

"We brought you here," King Emerson continues, no amount of sarcasm missing from his words, "because you've been hunting hybrids and capturing them."

I furrow my brow. "The hybrids? That's why I'm here?"

"Yes," Lorenzo takes over. "Our information states you've caught three of them without dying."

I nod. "Do you know where they're from?"

"No. We want to hire you to find out where the hybrids are from, to hunt them privately for us. You can work alongside your division if you wish, but this would be a private matter for you and not to be discussed with anyone," Lorenzo explains.

I look at the king, who is sitting with his arms crossed, watching me with the same bored expression he had when he got in here. He kidnapped me to ask for my help. I almost laugh. "Why would I do that? I don't want to help you and end up killed by the Fae Queen. She would kill me for even considering helping you."

The king tilts his head to the side. "You have a ward, do you not?"

"Yes," I bite out.

Zurine places her hand on my arm, and I nearly jump. "What my king suggests is that the young boy who you look after and his mother in the medical sleep might do well if you took our job. It is a job, not a favor, and you will be heavily paid."

King Emerson slides his eyes to me. "Find out who did this and find the hybrids' leader, and we will pay you an exorbitant amount. So much coin that you can move out of that hovel you live in and buy somewhere nice to live out your mortal life. Do we have a deal?"

I feel like King Emerson might not have heard this word often in his life, but here goes... "No."

His eyes narrow into sharp blades. "You would let your ward and his mother suffer? You would let the hybrids continue to rip apart your fellow mortals, out of what? Pride?"

I glare right back as I stand up and place my hands on the table. "I would do anything for Louie and my foster mom, but helping you will end up getting me killed. I'm not stupid. It's why you're asking me in the first place. Because you can't search in Ethereal City. The Fae Queen—"

He frowns and cuts me off midsentence. "You're a coward, Calliophe Sprite. How disappointing."

"Calliophe, we will protect you from the queen and her spies in the city," Zurine softy warns as I sit down . "Yes, there is a risk, and it is your choice. We are not here to force you into helping us."

Lorenzo looks at the king, and some kind of silent message seems to spread between them before he speaks. "You will receive ten percent of the million coins we will pay you. You will get the other ninety percent when you find out who they are. If you're not dead, that is."

A million coins. By the goddess. With that sort of money, I could wake my foster mom and take them both to live happily in Junepit City for the rest of our lives. I wouldn't have to wake up at the crack of dawn every day, fight and risk my life for scraps of coins to get us by. I could live and choose a real future for myself that isn't just a life I have to live to survive. All of it lies right in front of me, as risky as it is. Also, this is the closest I have ever gotten to finding out who the monster is that hunted me as a child and killed everyone I ever loved back then.

"But if I die," I say, leaning forward, "it's all for nothing, and my ward is left alone. I have too much to lose. Find someone else."

"I knew the mortal would be too selfish to do this," Julian sneers. "If we—"

King Emerson cuts him off. "We are not discussing that option again, Julian. Your anger with mortals clouds your judgment."

I rub my forehead. "Why do you want to know who is making the hybrids? How does it affect you?"

King Emerson barely even glances at me as Lorenzo answers. "We want to know because they took one of our people. Our sister, the princess of our race. She was taken three days ago, and we can't find her."

I look between King Emerson and Lorenzo... who never mentioned he is a prince. "Our sister?"

Emerson's eyes are like icy frost blowing over my skin with pepper sweet kisses. "Is there a problem?"

I'm in too deep because I'm actually considering this. Nerelyth is going to drown me in the seas when she hears about all of this. "How old is your sister? Why would they take her? How was she taken exactly?"

King Emerson looks like he has won, and I hate it. "She's young, nearly your age, and inexperienced in combat. They came, and they took her when we were away. Those left killed at least twenty of the hybrids, but there were endless amounts of them. They knew how to get in, where to find her, and how to get her out without alerting many."

I point out the obvious. "Someone fed them information, then?"

"My people are bound to me and cannot betray the royal blood. Whoever it is must have walked these halls at some time. Perhaps when my father or grandfather ruled the Forgotten City," he informs me.

Lorenzo's chair groans as he moves. "We want her back alive and will pay you. What have you to lose?"

I hate that he has a point in a way, but this is a risk. I'll be working with monsters to hunt down a bigger monster.

I sigh. "Why bother kidnapping me and not just asking me nicely back at my home?"

Emerson doesn't look remotely sorry. "Because you'll be staying here. It's safer for you while you are under our protection and working for us."

"I really don't think so. If you want me to work on this case, I'll need to be in Ethereal City, not here in the mountains. Plus, people are going to realize I'm missing, and that's going to draw attention," I counter. "I will take this job, but the condition is that I stay in my apartment."

He throws his own condition right back at me. "For the week. The weekends you spend here."

"Fine." I grit my teeth. The weekends, I can spend investigating the Wyerns and who might want to hunt down me.

He crosses his thick arms. "There was never an option. You work for me or you die."

"You're not my king," I remind him. "But I'm no coward, and I will find your sister. I want to stop whoever is creating the hybrids just as much as you. They are killing innocent mortals and supernaturals. This is my work, and you're right, I'm damn good at it."

His lips tilt up. "Still a coward under all that pretty pink hair. Pretending to be brave won't stop that fear in your chest from crawling itself out."

"Says the heartless monster king on a cold throne, hidden in a corner of the world, asking a mortal to help him because no one else would dare."

The room goes deadly silent.

Shit. Maybe I shouldn't have said that. I don't have it in me to apologize, but there is a little fear that crawls up my throat with how Emerson's eyes narrow on me. He looks at Lorenzo. "Have her trailed in the day, and one of us sleeps at hers at night. She is not to be left alone."

I want to argue I can look after myself, but the truth is, if the hybrids are working in groups, I'll take whatever protection I can get.

They can take the bumpy sofa and deal with my psychotic bat roommate.

She loves guests. Not.

Lorenzo nods sharply. "I'll arrange it all, brother."

"Everyone leave. Except you, Doe."

My eyes widen as they all stand and leave, and I don't even try to stand up. Lorenzo pats my back once before leaving. I assume it's some sort of good luck pat. I keep my eyes on the king, my hands gripping the seat of the chair tightly as he stands up and walks around the table. When the throne room doors are shut, he pushes the chair to my right aside and sits on the edge of the table next to me, his wing brushing so close it could touch my hand.

I lift my head. "What else do you want?"

He leans down, leaving our faces inches apart. This close, I can only smell how good his scent is and see how the leathers are tight across his body, his face smooth and sculpted into perfection. He is a beautiful monster indeed. "If you're caught by any fae, you do not mention my name. You do not tell a single fae a word of this, or I'll kill you myself. Do you understand?"

"Threats are idle. If a fae knew of this, I'd be dead way before you'd get to me."

And I'd be thankful for it, I bet.

His eyes seem to swirl like rippling water. Still shallow water that you'd walk into, unaware of the current underneath waiting to snatch you up. "Watch your back, mortal. Make one wrong step, and death will seem like a mercy."

My heart is racing fast as he leans back and then pushes off the table before walking away. Only when he is gone do I remember to breathe.

CHAPTER 5

"*T*hat went well, I trust."

I turn to face Lorenzo as I step out of the throne room, happy to escape that place after being stuck in there all day. He is waiting out in the corridor for me, his arms crossed as he leans against the wall. "Is he always like that?"

Lorenzo sighs and straightens. He may not look much like his brother, but he holds himself in a similar way, and now that I know, I can see some shared features. "Yes. I'm the fun brother, and Emerson is... well, he was brought up to be king. You don't stay king of the Wyerns without being ruthless."

I don't know what to say to that, and thankfully,

Lorenzo changes the subject. "Ready to go back to Ethereal City?"

I nod with a shiver. "Yes, but I don't look forward to flying back."

"Flying is the dramatic way to travel that far," Lorenzo tells me with a secretive curve of his lips. "The mirrors take about five hours to travel through, but it feels like minutes for us. So you'll be home just before the sun sets, I bet."

"Mirrors?" I ask with a frown.

He ignores me and walks away, and I'm left with no choice but to follow after him. "As I'm sleeping over, does that mean I get invited into your bed?"

I nearly choke on thin air. "Absolutely not."

"Damn. We're not allowed to touch you, but I've always been interested in forbidden things," he says.

"Forbidden by who?"

He pushes a door open, and I step into another corridor. By the goddess, this place is a maze. "Emerson. The moody git doesn't want anyone touching you and distracting you from your job. A waste, as our sleepovers could be so much more interesting and fun."

"I'm not interested, Lorenzo," I bluntly tell him.

He pretends to stab himself in the chest. "How will I survive now?"

I roll my eyes at his dramatics, even as I smile. This monster is funny at least, and I can rule him out of my list of who is my monster. He doesn't have wings. I wonder why for a moment, before he opens a door to a small room full of glowing mirrors. Mirrors fill every wall, each one of them encased in a gold frame. The floors are shiny, reflecting my image like the mirrors, and it's very warm in here, which is strange, as magic always feels like ice. There is magic in the air, strange and different from what I felt before, and Lorenzo closes the door behind us. "Welcome to the Speculis. One of our greatest secrets."

"Is this how you get the mortals I saw here?"

"Yes, and fae, sirens, and especially the Snake females. They are great with their tongu—"

"I don't need to know that," I cut him off.

He grins. "Fine, but yes. We always keep them blindfolded and wipe their memories before they go back. Before you ask, they always are aware of what they are agreeing to when coming here. Most beg."

Goose bumps litter my skin. "What do your females say?"

"Considering there are three female Wyerns left —they are very rare—not much. They have their own males for fun."

"Three? That's it?" I whisper.

"Shit. Don't repeat that," he says, rubbing his face. "Solandis being taken is messing with my head."

"Your sister was named after the dragon goddess?" I quietly ask, feeling his sorrow like it's my own for a moment. If Louie were taken, I'd do anything to get him back.

He waves his hand across the mirror and offers me his other hand. "Yes. She was born on Nocturno."

The Falling Night.

"So was I."

He looks right at me as I take his hand and frowns. "How unusual. Solandis would like you."

I don't know why I shared that. It's one of the only things I know about myself, from my limited records. Nocturno is the middle point of the year, a special day because the sun never rises in the sky and it's an eternal night. The old fairy tale used to explain this annual occurrence is that Nocturno was the day the dragon goddess died, and when her spirit left this world, the sun grieved and did not appear. Instead, the night sky burned with a million stars and the moons shone brighter than ever.

He takes a step towards the mirror, and I tighten my grip on his hand, which is soft. "Don't let go."

I barely get a second to brace myself as Lorenzo tugs me straight into the mirror, and we fall through it like it's thick water. I can't breathe, the warm magic suffocating me, and I start to panic even as Lorenzo's hand tightly pulls me along. Whatever this magic is, it's old and horrible, painting itself against my skin.

Suddenly, the magic disappears, and I gasp for air as we both stumble out into the street outside my apartment building. I look behind me at the wall, which is shimmering with gold magic right before it slowly fades away into nothing but stone.

"That was incredibly horrible."

"The first time is always the worst," he says with a teasing grin.

I chuckle and pull my hand away.

He smiles. "Oh, I thought we'd hold hands forever."

"I'm sure you can find another, more willing mortal to hold your hand," I dryly reply.

He winks at me. "Usually I like them to hold other things of mine."

I walked right into that one. I shake my head as I walk away and head into my apartment, noticing Lorenzo is right, and it's already night out. He strolls in after me, and I glance around, noticing a few people on the streets. Thankfully, none of them pay much attention as we head inside and up the stairs.

Lorenzo hands me keys halfway up. "Thanks. My weapons?"

"Emerson has them," he replies with a shrug.

I sigh. "You need to be careful while you're here in the city. Any supernatural is going to know what you are."

"They won't see me. I can fade away into shadows, and I'm damn good at it. It's why I'm here with you," he replies, taking the steps two at a time and getting ahead of me. Show off. "It's a royal gift."

"So not all Wyerns can do it?" I ask. I'm surprised it's so quiet in the building, and we are lucky we haven't passed anyone on the way up.

"No, but some of the powerful can use magic to hide themselves for a time."

I nod, all of a sudden feeling very tired, and the day is catching up to me. I keep quiet as I climb the rest of the stairs, glancing at Louie's floor as we pass it by. He won't find it suspicious. I haven't seen him today. He'll just think I'm out hunting monsters again... but the boss won't think the same thing. He is going to kill me. I'll just have to make it up that I was sick or something. Nerelyth can help me come up with something. We are good at covering each other's back. She's definitely going to notice that I didn't turn up for her birthday though, and I'm sure she is worried. Stress starts building into a headache as I get to my apartment door and unlock it. I head inside, clicking my fingers to turn the lights on as Lorenzo shuts the door behind us.

"So, where is my room?"

"Prince Lorenzo, here is your luxury bed," I sarcastically say, waving at the sofa. "I do hope it meets your high standards."

He laughs deeply behind me as I open my cupboards to find a snack, disappointingly finding them empty. Oh well, it's not the first time I haven't eaten for a whole day.

Posy flies in the room, hooking her claws onto the top of the counter and hanging upside down as she inspects us. "Of course you brought the bat back with you."

"Technically, you're more a bat than I," Lorenzo

smoothly says and looks at me. "As children, we used to chase bats like this for sport. Why do you keep it here?"

"She's a mortal cursed to be a bat forever," I explain with a sigh. "Because of her sassy attitude, I bet."

I don't actually know why Posy was cursed, or by who. I found her injured and alone years ago, and I felt sorry for her. It's been something I've grown to regret over the years. I hoped she would turn back and the curse would end. It didn't.

Posy's sweet, innocent little eyes look at me and, sometimes, when she doesn't speak, she looks very cute. Other times when she does speak, I'm tempted to throw her out of the window.

"This is Lorenzo, Posy. He'll be staying here tonight. In fact, we'll have more guests over than usual at night. It's part of a new job that I've taken."

"No," Posy snarkily replies.

I cross my arms. "You don't have a choice."

"I'm your roommate, and I don't agree to your bat fuck buddies moving in here."

"It's not exactly like you actually pay for anything! Remember, I pay for your food, this place and everything else. Try being grateful for once. Did you even notice I was kidnapped?"

She rolls her eyes. "Kidnapped? Sure. You're very overdramatic."

"Posy," I sigh in annoyance. "I just—"

She interrupts me. "The monster bat clearly didn't satisfy you. Is this why you have a new lover? He might not have wings, but he smells like a bat; still your thing, it seems. If you come back in this lovely, bitchy mood of yours after he is done, then there is no fixing you."

I shake my head. I'm too tired to deal with her tonight. Lorenzo is trying not to chuckle and failing.

"I like you, bat mortal," he exclaims as he strolls to the sofa, and it actually collapses under the weight of him because it's such a crappy sofa.

"Help yourself to whatever food you can find, which won't be a lot," I tell him as I walk past. "I'm going to sleep. Night."

"Good night, Calliophe."

Shutting the door behind me, I walk over to my bed and sit down on it, just where Emerson sat before, and his scent is still lingering in here. It reminds me he had my romance book, and as I look over at my side unit, I realize it's missing. He took it. Dammit. I was only halfway through it, and it was getting to the good part. After stripping my clothes and throwing them in the sink, I use enchanted soap to instantly clean my clothes before I hang them up to dry.

After having a shower, I get back into my worn purple pajama top and shorts before climbing into bed. As soon as my head hits the pillow, I fall asleep. Morning light trickles in through the window, waking me, and I sit up wondering if it's all a dream as I smell bacon. We don't have money for bacon. I walk out of my bedroom, rubbing my eyes as my stomach rumbles loudly. I'm surprised to see a very shirtless Lorenzo in my kitchen... cooking.

"I hope you like bacon, eggs, and pancakes. I got everything from the market this morning. You were right. Your ice storage and cupboards have shitloads of nothing in them. No wonder you're so thin. Sit down, I'm cooking you breakfast."

I'm speechless enough that I sit down at the counter in a bit of a daze. A few minutes later, a plate of food is pushed in front of me, and my mouth waters. I'm used to buying scraps of meat, fruit that is borderline moldy, and anything cheap enough for me to afford. These are more expensive, rare even, and the spices alone would have cost me an entire month's wage. Fluffy pancakes, bright fruits and bacon are piled on my plate, and I gulp as I cut a piece up.

"Thank you," I tell Lorenzo just before I take a bite. By the goddess, I forgot how good food is supposed to taste.

"I've changed my mind. Lorenzo is very welcome here," Posy announces behind me. I turn to see her sitting in a fluffy pink bed with a pile of expensive meat sticks she is chewing on. What the fuck? She looks at me in disgust. "You, on the other hand, are not. Haven't you got work or anywhere else to be?"

"Good morning to you too," I mutter, turning back to my food.

Posy likes Lorenzo... I wasn't sure she ever liked anyone. Even when Louie is here, she mostly just ignores him, and she hates Nerelyth with a passion. Lorenzo has a plate piled high with food as he sits on the stool next to me and begins to eat in silence.

I'm having breakfast with a Wyern. How is this my life now?

I ignore her to dig into my breakfast, and by the time I'm done, I find Lorenzo has easily eaten twice as much as me.

"That was really nice. Thank you again."

He looks at me and smiles. "Ah, so you have manners when you have been fed."

I smile back. "I'm going to get dressed, but I have a question," I say. "Why did the king come to get me and not you? Or a member of the court, when it's so dangerous for you to be here."

He doesn't look at me as he replies. "When it comes to my brother, rules and laws are nothing but sticks to break as he walks over them."

"Fine, but your sister is missing, and honestly, you don't seem that bothered by it. Neither does your court."

This time, he turns and his eyes meet mine. "The court are not supporters of Solandis, and most are likely happy she is gone. She believed we shouldn't hide in the mountains anymore as outcasts and monsters to those who know only the truth of the fae. That the old laws should be forgotten and war should begin. Many of us do not want a war, and she made no qualms in telling everyone she came across how cowardly she thought they were. Solandis is my half-sister and very much like her mother, who was hated by the court in the end."

Ah, so not the king's full-blooded sister either, by the sounds of it. Where are their parents? Are they still alive? I can't believe they wouldn't have been in the talk with me about their missing daughter if they were alive. I wish I knew more rumors about the Wyerns. Maybe Nerelyth will.

"Why?"

"There will be another time for that story," he replies, going back to his food and digging his fork into a red fruit. "Wherever my sister is, you're our best chance of finding her. Ethereal City has its secrets, and so do we. Find them, Calliophe."

"I'm telling my partner everything, and she won't tell a soul. Also, I want my money now. The ten percent I was promised," I say, placing my hands on my hips.

He nods at my bookcase, where a pile of gold papers line the one shelf. A hundred thousand, I bet. My mouth goes dry as I walk over, letting the shadows of the corridor cover me as I touch the money for a moment. I look over at Lorenzo, who is still watching me, and he speaks before I can. "I can't approve of you telling the siren this. My king will not be happy."

"Well, he isn't here, is he?" I counter, lowering my hand and hating how vulnerable I felt and looked at that moment. I've never seen money like that. The security it could bring Louie. I won't have to worry about him all of the time. That money is a life for me. A life away from the dreads of Ethereal City.

Smiling, I wipe a few tears away as I go to my room, shut the door and mentally shake myself. I have to get to work. I get dressed in my leathers, clipping two daggers to both my thighs and lacing my enchanted rope around my stomach. Lastly, I put on my leather coat and tie my pink hair up in a high ponytail, leaving a few strands out before going back into the living room and slipping on my boots. I go back to the shelf and grab a bunch of gold papers, tucking some into my boots along with my keys in my back pocket before facing Lorenzo, who has cleaned up and is now sitting on the sofa, Posy sleeping curled up in her bed like a cat.

"See you later. There is a key in the bathroom, under the white stone by the sink. Lock up before you leave," I say.

"I won't be here tonight, but someone will," he replies, spreading his long arms out. "Going to miss me?"

Truthfully—yes. I like having breakfast made for me and having someone here Posy doesn't ignore or hate other than me. "No."

He laughs, climbing up and handing me a large envelope. "In here is a painting of my sister. There's also various things that we've done to look at the hybrids that we killed. Details about them, what we suspect they were before they were changed into hybrids. Just random things I've found and information from our spies in the city on the hybrids they have encountered."

"Thanks. It will help," I reply, taking it from him and tucking it under my arm. He touches my shoulder before I walk away, and I look back at him.

He crosses his beefy arms. "You'll be watched, and if you're in trouble, just call for help. Someone will come and help."

"I can handle myself. Thanks."

I feel his eyes on me as I walk away. "I'm over a hundred and four years old, Calliophe, and even I would take caution with this."

I look back at him, nodding once before leaving him in my apartment.

I feel full, unsurprisingly, as I head down the stairs to Louie's apartment, heading inside with the key hidden in the flower pot outside. He is at school or on his way there, and I quickly check on my foster mom before leaving ten gold notes and a quick letter explaining not to go crazy with it and I'll explain later. A hundred thousand isn't enough to wake up his mom, but two hundred thousand would be.

I can do this.

For Louie.

For my foster mom and everything I owe her.

Locking up, I leave her apartment and take the twenty-minute walk back to the Enforcer Guild, hoping it doesn't rain. I rush up the steps as thunder echoes in the distance, and I'm not too surprised to find Nerelyth waiting outside for me, fully dressed in black leathers that match mine and her boots with daggered heels. I need to borrow those boots. Well, borrow and never give back until she steals them back. Her arms are tightly crossed, her red hair braided back, and she looks furious as she taps her foot on the stone as I rush up to her.

"What the hell happened to you? First with my birthday and not turning up and then you don't turn up for work? I tried your apartment, but I only found Posy and her random chatter about monster fucking," she rants, her eyes slightly glowing and her skin near shining with her power. "I was really getting worried, Calli. For a second, I even thought about singing in every part of the city until I found you."

She flings her arms around me and squeezes me

tight. "I was always told not to be friends with mortals, and then you turned up, pink hair and all, and you're my best friend. You can't disappear like that."

She whacks me on the arm as she steps back. "Ouch, but I love you too, bestie. Can I talk now and explain?"

"Did you really fuck a monster?"

"Posy is insane," I mutter, noticing the guards are listening in, and one of them has very red cheeks. "We should go and talk somewhere else."

"Gotcha," she nods in agreement, hooking her arm through mine as we walk in. We both say hello to Wendy before going through past both of our offices, which are nothing more than small desks in box rooms, and into the interrogation room. The soundproof room is bright, and it takes a second to adjust my eyes to the light as I lock the door behind us.

Nerelyth perches on the table as I start explaining everything that happened. By the end, her mouth is wide open, and she's utterly speechless.

Sagging after unloading all that, I lean against the wall. "I'm really fucked, aren't I?"

"They are Wyerns...," she whispers, clearly shocked.

"If I don't find this princess or solve this hybrid case, I think that the king might actually kill me," I say, rubbing my head. Another headache is already building. I used to get them a lot as a kid, but I haven't had any in years. I'll have to stop off at the healers on the way home tonight. Maybe stress brings them on... not that I'm usually stress free.

"They're not going to kill you. I won't let them," she says fiercely. "And it doesn't matter. We will find this princess and who is making the hybrids."

"Thank you," I softly say, feeling like a weight has been lifted from my shoulders by just telling her this all and knowing she has my back. "I'm surprised you even believe me. It sounds like a crazy nightmare."

"Even you, my friend, are not creative enough to make this up," she says with a small laugh. "And I'm happy to know you didn't pick up a male who looks like a monster for a one-night stand. Posy had me worried about your judgment for a second there."

I laugh, shaking my head. "Posy actually likes the prince who slept on my sofa last night."

"I'm not sure many can say they had a Wyern King kidnap them and a Wyern Prince sleeping over," she says with a smile that drops for a moment. "It's going to be okay. The money... you need it for Louie and his mom. For you to finally get out of this dump."

"I'll share it with you for helping," I say quickly.

"No," she sharply replies with an echo of power in her voice that laces a chill down my spine.

My eyes widen, and she looks away for a moment.

I clear my throat. "Okay, but the offer is there. Partners for life?"

"Always," she replies with a sad smile. "Sorry, I shouldn't have snapped like that."

"One day, if you ever want to tell me your secrets, I'll listen," I reply, pushing off the wall. "No pressure."

"Maybe one day," she repeats. "By the way, the boss has called a meeting. He was really pissed that you weren't here yesterday. I told him that you were sick, but I don't think he bought it."

"He wouldn't," I mutter. "He was mad about the hybrid and gave me a big lecture."

"It's a damn shame he talks so much with that pretty face of his."

I chuckle and look at the door. "Do you think there is any way he will believe the sick story from me?"

"Nope," she quietly replies, coming over and resting her head on my shoulder for a moment. "But screw him. You've done worse than missing a day of work, and he hasn't fired you yet."

True. Very true. I unlock the door, and we both head out together, passing the offices before making our way upstairs to the boss's floor and greeting a few enforcers we pass. There are at least fifteen enforcers already here, many looking bored as they wait around the room for the boss. We take a space beside the window, and I cross my arms as more enforcers flock into the room and fill the space.

About ten minutes later, the boss walks in, and even his footsteps seem moody. He looks around the room and pauses when he finds me. For a moment, I think he looks relieved before his lips turn into a thin line and he looks away. I don't miss the disappointment before he does. The boss isn't alone. All I see is blond hair over the whispering crowd before he stops next to my boss, and Merrick nods at him. He's fae, the newcomer. His crystal blue eyes, pointed ears, and the posh forest green uniform make it clear he is one of the queen's army, along with the royal sigil on his arm and the deadly green-bladed sword strapped on to his back. Not that he needs weapons to kill us all. His skin shimmers with power, like the glittering sea when the sun is at its highest.

"What's he doing here?" Nerelyth whispers to me.

Whatever it is, I have a bad feeling about this.

"Everyone quiet," the boss demands, and we all go silent. "This is the commander of the Queen's Royal Army. Commander Trask."

Everyone goes silent for an entirely different reason. "The commander here has a mission for us all. It's very important, so I suggest you listen."

He steps forward and puts his hands on the chair in front of him, leaning forward to look at all of us. His eyes flicker on me for a moment before continuing on until he has looked at us all. I wonder if he can see into our souls. I'm sure it's just a rumor I've heard about the great commander of the queen's armies. "As you all are aware, there are new monsters in the city. Hybrids. They're dangerous. They've killed many mortals there, causing havoc, and last night, they broke into one of the Royal

Cities. They kidnapped the queen's grandson, who's ill equipped to fight."

I look at Nerelyth, who looks as shocked as me. "They came in a massive group and killed many fae. Those who were attacked were all young, and it was a party full of females and males that do not fight. They were completely outnumbered. The news will be spread throughout Ethereal City by midday, but until then, you are not to speak of this."

Deaths of any fae are seen as a great tragedy to our world. There will be mourning funerals across the entire city for months. "Why are you telling us this?"

I glance at the male enforcer who asked, one I don't know, at the same time everyone else does. He goes as red as his hair, but the commander answers, "Each one of you is going to be sent out to look for who created the hybrids. Who's leading them and why? Anyone that finds out or rescues the queen's grandson will be rewarded with more money than they can possibly imagine and invited into the dream palaces for the rest of their lives. Along with their families and loved ones and friends."

Whispers spread like wildfire around the enforcers, but my tongue feels like lead. "Now I will leave you to it. Your boss has any information you need. There will be more fae about in the city for a while, and they will assist you if needed. Be aware that the queen's grandson is clearly a very desired prize by many outside this city, and others will be searching for him for their own reasons."

He looks right at me, his midnight eyes sharpening before he turns and leaves.

Everyone is talking between themselves as I turn to Nerelyth, and she looks as pale as me. What are the odds of the Fae Queen wanting the same thing that the Wyern King does?

They both have loved ones missing, and they both need our help.

Made in the USA
Coppell, TX
20 November 2024

40587621R00204